KILL FOR YOU

CJ MORROW

Tamarillas Press

This book is written in British English.

Cover image: istockphoto.com
Cover design: © CJ Morrow 2022

ISBN: 978-1-913807-32-0

This book is dedicated, as usual, to my family. They know who they are.

Books by CJ MORROW

Women's Fiction/Romantic Comedy:
Save the Date
Escape to Christmas Cottage
It's Pamela Rigby Actually
Sooo Not Looking for a Man
We Can Work it Out
Little Mishaps and Big Surprises
Mermaid Hair and I Don't Care
Blame it on the Onesie
A Onesie is not just for Christmas

Psychological Thriller:
Never Leaves Me
Kill For You

Fantasy:
The Finder
The Illusionist
The Sister
The Family

Party Time

One

ANGIE

My brother, what can I say about him? The most talented man I've ever known. And the funniest and the kindest. And clever.

Adam Hames RA, you've probably heard of him. No? Maybe you don't move in those circles, I know I don't, but you'll have seen his work. It sells for the kind of money I could never afford, so out of reach to us mere mortals. But you will have seen his paintings, you probably have one in your own home in one form or another. You don't believe me?

Adam was talented from the very beginning, probably even before he emerged red and angry from our mother's womb. Probably talented at conception. The baby who should never have been.

I was our parents' fourth child, three boisterous boys preceded me, rampaging around the house and causing the kind of mayhem and wreckage that only three boys can. There's George, Henry and William, the gap between me and William, the youngest of my older brothers, is five years. The gap between George and William is five years too, and slotted neatly in between them is Henry. Our parents were always going to stop at three, but my mother wanted a girl and persuaded my somewhat reluctant father to try again.

I often wonder how many more tries she would have made had she only had boys, but fortunately, I was a girl. The perfect kind too, blonde haired, blue-eyed, peachy perfect. They called me Angelique because I looked so angelic. I prefer Angie which goes better with my now dark hair, funny how things change. There were no plans for any more children after me, none whatsoever.

Adam arrived two weeks early and a mere eleven months after me. My mother stayed in hospital a little longer after having him so that she could *have her tubes tied*. She wasn't going to chance another surprise. Five children were more than enough, thank you.

Due to the small age gap Adam and I were close. I was so young when he was born that I cannot remember a time without him. Because of the close gap and when our birthdays fell, we started school together and we were in the same school year. My parents insisted, mainly because Adam and I demanded, that we were in the same class and start school at the same time, something the school wasn't keen on, but, if you know my mother, you'd know that arguing with her would be pointless.

We were what some called Irish twins, born less than a year apart. A term that puzzled us as, even at the ages of four and five, we knew we weren't Irish, we knew we weren't twins. Not that it mattered, people could call us what they liked, we didn't value other people's opinions of our relationship, not even then.

Right from the beginning Adam was the clever one, despite being younger he learnt to read first, he could hold a pencil, then a pen, then a paintbrush almost as soon as he could sit up. Numbers came easily to him, counting to one hundred was his party piece even before starting school.

His talent was prodigious right from the beginning, while the rest of the class were drawing stick men he was drawing facial features, clear and recognisable. A teacher once used the term genius to describe him, though never about me.

We went through primary school together, and while I had my own friends, girls like me, he never found his crew and was always content to hang around with me and my friends. He was popular with them too, possibly more popular than I was. Sometimes, even though I loved him, I disliked my little brother.

By senior school though still in the same registration group we were in different sets for subjects. He sailed through maths lessons and later spent his time explaining equations and probability to me when we both knew it should probably have been the other way around, with me being the oldest. But truly, it never mattered. We were close. Thick as thieves our mother used to say. We covered for each other. We lied for each other. We used to say we would die for each other – but that was during the dramatic teenage years when hormones fuelled our emotions.

By the time we did our GCSE's Adam had already sold a painting. Admittedly it was to his art teacher, but she paid him real money for it – a shrewd investment for her, as it turned out. By the time we were in college, he had sold several others and had been approached by *IKEA* to produce artwork to sell in their stores. Off the back of that *Next* approached him to design greetings cards, closely followed by other companies. See, I bet you have one in your house, or have received one of his birthday cards. By the time he was eighteen he had a regular income from his art and he'd only just passed his A levels. He made it all look so easy.

Was I jealous of him? No, for the most part I basked in his reflected glory. I was Adam's sister, everyone wanted to be my friend so that they could get close to him. It was fun.

We were both devastated at our separation when he left to go to art school in London. I couldn't go with him, I had no talent for art, obviously. I enrolled on a marketing course locally but spent most of my weekends in London with Adam. Because he already had a steady and growing income, he never had the burden of a student loan and he was able to afford a charming, if modest, flat near the art school, no mucking-in in dingy student digs for him. Maybe that was the mistake, not slumming it with the others, it meant he was separate, alone. That said he was always popular with his fellow students, but he never really mixed with them away from classes. And, of course, he had Jasper by then.

Those were the days, our halcyon days, as he called them. I had to go and look that up after he'd said it, I didn't want to show my ignorance, even then, by asking him. He wouldn't have laughed at me, but I would have cringed.

He was a lot to live up to, my brother, Adam Hames RA.

☯☯☯

My parents walk in together, shuffle to the front seats. God, they look old. And grey. Their faces have a bleached, waxen look about them. I suppose they are old; our mother had her seventieth a few months ago, that was the last time we saw Adam. Our father is five years older than her, but they look older today. Black does not suit them, either of them. I think I wear it well, but they definitely don't. Is that an age thing?

I smile over at her, well, I pull the sides of my mouth up, more a grimace really, and she stares straight through me. But Dad sees me and nods. The bags under his eyes are getting bigger. He's had a haircut, especially for today, probably.

He still works, my dad, although he's cut his hours to the minimum. He works with my brothers, all three of them, in their family firm of solicitors. They offered me a job there once, after I'd finished my marketing course. I turned it down, I didn't want to be a receptionist. I do wonder at my folly because they would have paid me more than my current marketing assistant job does, or any of the previous ones, I suspect.

Gray puts his hand on mine and squeezes.

I grip it back then let go. Get off me. It's good of him to be here really; he's here purely as my support, he's never even met Adam. I told him not to come. I let him off. After all we've only been together a short while. No one would judge him for his absence, but he insisted.

Now he's irritating me with his sympathetic face and soft words of comfort.

'Okay?' he asks, his voice little above a whisper.

I nod. Of course I'm not okay. How could I be okay? Ever. Again.

The place is full. The side we're on full of family, my parents, me and Gray, my older brothers' families, our aunts, uncles, cousins. We're a big extended family and they're all here today. I recognise everyone, their faces so very familiar. I recognise them all because it's hardly any time since we were all together for Mum's giant birthday party.

On the other side many of the faces are familiar. There's Rue, her hair deep purple today, her eyes red-rimmed, which is not unusual for Rue given how much *charlie* she snorts. There's Brent, he's wearing a tartan suit, admittedly it's dark, green and black, but it's still tartan – I think that's disrespectful. Brent is now completely bald, the last time I saw him he was still sporting that monk look with an odd comb over to the front, gelled forward pretending to be a fringe. Evidently, he's given that up, wise decision. I can see Jasper's grey quiff and, as I lean forward I get a good look at his face, gone is the weird goatee beard he had the last time I saw him. God, he's aged a lot recently and he seems to have acquired himself a look-alike boyfriend. There's Mel and Zoe and Bill and Joe. So many more I half know, their faces familiar, their names a blur.

I scan the rows looking for *him*, the elusive Perry. Not that I truly know what Perry looks like as I've never met him in person, yet I believe I'll know him if I see him. Will I? He's drop dead gorgeous, that's how Adam always described him. And tall. And very blonde, this I know because I once saw the back of his head during a *Facetime* call. I also saw his face but by then he had moved far enough away that it was blurred and out of focus. He waved to me at Adam's instruction.

I'm not really expecting him to turn up, but you never can tell with people.

'Any sign of Perry?' Gray asks, echoing my thoughts.

I shrug my response. I can't speak. I have to hold it together today.

The music starts, it's sombre, not the sort of thing Adam would have chosen, I'm sure. But he didn't choose, did he? Mum did. And the music reflects her misery not his joy for living.

Some people glance back towards the doors. I can't. Gray leans over me a little and peers that way. I push him away by wriggling my shoulders.

I think I may dump Gray after this is over.

They're progressing down the aisle – is that the right word in a crematorium, aisle? I suppose it is. The coffin is sleek and black and must have cost a fortune, but Adam could afford it, and he will be paying for it though not up front, it'll come out of his estate. He wasn't of an age to invest in advance in his own funeral plan like our Gran did, any more than I am. According to the funeral directors she had the funeral she always wanted. Whatever the hell that means.

George, Henry and William, together with three of the funeral company's staff are carrying the coffin. The brothers insisted even though the funeral director suggested, preferred indeed, to push the coffin along on a trolley. I insisted I wanted to carry the coffin too, but at five-foot-two it wasn't practical; my brothers are six-foot-plus, just like Adam was. Imagine me running along with my hands in the air trying to hold on. The thought amuses me and I let out a little snort of amusement which Gray misinterprets causing him to reach for my hand again. I pull it away.

I can't bear to think of Adam inside that coffin. His fair, curly hair resting on the pillow, his artist's hands folded in front of him. I wonder if they managed to get all the paint out from under his nails? Did they even try? I'll never know. We were discouraged from visiting his lifeless body in the chapel of rest – too much damage they said. Just as well; I know what he looked like, what he should have looked like, that's the image I want to keep in my head, not how he probably looks now. Mangled.

I pull in a deep breath and let it out slowly. I can't bear it.

Gray twitches, moves a hair's breadth closer to me, I shudder and move away.

The dirge music continues, the procession moves past us. George, my oldest brother who is now pushing forty-seven, winces as he passes. He has a longstanding back injury and the weight of that coffin cannot be doing it any good. I watch him swallow as he moves on past.

Finally they reach the plinth, the one in front of the little curtain which will open before the bowels of the place swallow up my darling little brother.

My big brothers take their places next to their wives.

Someone starts to talk. A minister? I don't know. Someone saying nice things about Adam.

At the front, to the right of the coffin is a self-portrait, in acrylics, of Adam. Painted just five years ago. It was a very good likeness of him at the time and because he was young and hasn't changed too much, it still is. That's what he looks like inside that coffin, or that's what I tell myself. I know it's not true. I glance over at it, dark and sleek with its top covered in white lilies. I can't bear it.

He gave the painting to me. Laughing, he said, 'Have this, it will be worth something in the future, look on it as your pension.'

I laughed back. I said, 'I can't take that.'

He shrugged. 'You can.'

'You haven't signed it.'

He grinned, took up a thick black marker and wrote *Portrait of the artist by the artist, Adam Hames RA*. He even dated it.

I sold it a few months back; I was between jobs and I desperately needed a decent car to get to interviews. It did fetch a good price but not as much as it would now, of course. His death has seen the price of his work soar. Well, there won't be any more, will there?

It's really good of the new owner to lend it to us for today. So kind.

There's some music and suddenly we're singing *All Things Bright and Beautiful*. What hell is this? I thought one of the advantages of not having a church service was not to sing hymns. Adam wasn't religious, he had no time for any of it. Our family isn't particularly religious. This will be Mum's doing, the all things bright and beautiful was Adam, her favourite son, the one that should never have been.

And now he isn't.

Two

And here we are, back at the family home.

It's a squeeze, despite it being a sizeable house with an enormous kitchen. I think everyone from the crematorium is here. Every last one.

'Rue,' I say, forcing a smile at her as she blinks back great globule tears. 'How are you?'

She nods and sniffs, she's probably wondering how long she can hold on before finding the toilet and going off for a snort or two of *charlie*.

'Been better,' she says, sniffing again, cuffing the tears on her cheeks with the back of her hands. She has a new tattoo, I notice; the ace of spades on the inside of her wrist. 'So sorry for your fam,' she adds.

I nod.

Gray snakes his arm around my waist and pulls me in tightly, attempts to steer me away from Rue.

I shake him off.

'Did you ever meet Perry' I ask her. 'Is he here?'

She shakes her head. 'Don't know. Never met him in person. Where's the loo?'

I point her in the direction of her next *charlie* snort and move onto Brent. 'Did you ever meet Perry?'

'No,' Brent says. 'The bastard. He should be here,

shouldn't he? Weren't they engaged? He's not here though, is he? I know everyone here, don't I? Even your family and there's no Perry.'

'Right. Okay.' Perry might be wandering around helping himself to the bought-in buffet and sipping the wine my parents have put out for all we know because no one seems to have met him. Or he could be in the loo snorting *charlie* with Rue, not that Rue would know, because her brain's so addled she probably wouldn't notice.

Gray puts his arm around me again and pulls me away from Brent, this time I don't object.

'Bit odd, isn't it, him not being here?' Gray says.

I shrug.

Across the room, leaning against the French windows, Jasper catches my eye. He raises a hand and offers a weak wave, then turns his eyes back to the windows, staring out, drink in hand. It was Jasper who was with Adam when it happened. Jasper is devastated about Adam on several levels. Adam was Jasper's best client, they were the best of friends, he identified the body – something we're all grateful for. He was a little bit in love with Adam.

'Hello, Angie,' Grace says. 'And you must be the elusive Gray.' She thrusts a hand across me to shake with Gray's.

He nods and smiles, strokes her hand and charms her instantly.

Grace is George's wife, the mother of his three daughters. All four women in that family are tall, blonde, willowy and beautiful.

Gray goes off to get us all drinks, Grace's idea.

'*He's* rather lovely,' she says, leaning in close to me. 'You've kept him well hidden.'

'Not really. Not known him long.'

'Good of him to come today then.' She nods her approval. 'He's charming and quite the looker. You should hang onto him.' She's right, I should. He is a looker. He's tall, his hair is neat and dark, including his perfectly trimmed beard, his manners perfect, his teeth even more perfect, he says all the right things at the right times even if I don't want to hear them. Physically, he's almost perfect, just that one little thing, when's he really tired his left eye wanders independent of the right. It's that little imperfection that makes him perfect. Maybe I won't dump Gray after all this is over.

'Did you ever meet Perry?' I ask. It's a very longshot, I know.

'Who?' she says, screwing up her beautiful face. 'I've never heard you mention a Perry, when was he your boyfriend?' Trust Grace, she wanders around with her head in the clouds. Adam certainly mentioned him enough times at our Mum's birthday party.

I shake my head slowly just as Gray returns, which Grace interprets as my reluctance to discuss a previous boyfriend in front of a current one.

'So, how long have you two been together?' Grace directs her question to Gray.

'Umm, almost two months now, isn't it, Angie?' He's cagey because we met online and I've told him not to tell my family that. We first met in person just a week or so before Adam died. Maybe that's why Gray irks me a little, because I connect his arrival with Adam's death. Ironically it was because of Adam that I joined the online dating scene again, because he had no room for me, because he was so wrapped up in Perry.

'Yes,' I say, taking a big swig of my drink. He's brought us red wine and it hits my throat like a foul-tasting medicine – I really don't like red wine, never drink the stuff but today I'll make an exception.

Grace takes a little sip of hers then puts it on a table. She's not going to make an exception.

I knock back the rest of my drink. 'Anyone for another?' I ask, but Grace and Gray are suddenly deep in conversation about local house prices, so I wander away and they don't even notice.

'When are you going to Adam's?' George's voice is right behind me.

I spin round to face him, my newly filled glass in hand.

'Hey, go easy on that stuff, we don't want a repeat of last week, do we?'

'Oh shut up,' I say, and take a deep gulp of wine - white now. I know it annoys him, my oldest brother; he's such a damn zealot these days. He used to love a glass or two, or three or four or more of wine, but he had to give up on health grounds. Now he's an insufferable teetotaller and a bore about it too. 'This is only my second, though why I'm justifying myself to you, I don't know.'

In response he does that thing with his eyebrows, raises them, then lowers his head and looks out of the top of his eyes. They all do that, my brothers, even Adam. I suppose they get it from Dad.

'Stop it,' I mutter. But I know why he's cautioning me. He can't take all that emotion. To be fair, I don't think I can either. We were supposed to be having a civilised, adult family dinner. Just Mum, Dad, the brothers and their wives, and me. It was the first time, no, the only time, that we'd all been together, just us. We were supposed to be honouring Adam, privately celebrating his life without the audience that would be at the funeral. So I drank too much, cried, accused them all of not understanding him, not appreciating him, not having a creative bone in their collective body… Well, I'm sure you get the picture. I was hysterical by the time George led me away from the table and out to his car. And I was asleep by the time we reached my home. I have little to no recollection of being helped into bed.

Perhaps George is right, we don't want a repeat of that situation.

'So,' he says, returning to his original question, 'when are you going to Adam's?'

'Monday, probably.'

'Is Gray going with you?'

'No.' I shake my head as if to say don't be so stupid. Not that Gray hasn't offered, he has, too many times.

'On your own?'

'Yep.' I glug back some more wine.

'Would you like me to come?'

'No, you're all right. I plan to stay until the job is done. I'll stay up there maybe a week or two.'

'What about your job?'

I give a little shrug. 'Got myself signed off with depression.'

'Oh.' He has that look on his face, judgemental.

'What? I am depressed. None of you understand quite how close me and Adam were, how much it hurts.'

George looks at me, his face blank, which I think rather proves my point. Then he says, 'He was my brother too.'

'Sorry.'

'The offer's still there, if you want help, just shout. I can come for the odd day. And we do all know exactly how close you two were, it's why he left you everything.' I'm not sure exactly how they all feel about that. Adam made a will about ten years ago, he'd never updated it, never changed it. Lodged with my brothers all this time, it's astonishingly simple, everything goes to me. Everything. He was nowhere near as famous and successful when he made that will as he is now.

'Thank you.' I lean over and hug him, my big brother.

'You'll need to see his accountant to go over the financials. I had a brief conversation with him, there are irregularities, but I'm sure you'll sort them out,' he says, while we're still hugging.

'Okay.'

'Ah, George, I've been looking for you.' Grace's voice cuts into our extended hug.

I pull away and smile at her. Gray, who is close behind Grace, smiles back at me.

'I was offering help to Angie… with Adam's place. She's going up on Monday.'

'I see. Well, he can't stay overnight, just so you know. Too many commitments at home.'

Out of Grace's sight George rolls his eyes at me and I laugh.

'I've offered to go, haven't I?' Gray's voice sounds petulant. 'Numerous times.'

I repeat the same answer to him that *I've* used numerous times, 'I need to do this on my own and you've never even met Adam. It would feel wrong.'

Gray does a little shrug and looks away, he's annoyed, but I can't help that. It's another of his perfect character traits, he's selfless and will help anyone with anything.

'I need to do this on my own,' I say again, then I turn around, refill my glass, and wander off in search of food. If I'm going to drink, and it seems I am, I should at least attempt to soak it up.

'Angie,' Rue yells, when I find a clean plate and start helping myself to buffet food. She puts herself far too close to me.

'Hi.' I lean around her to reach some salad, though what I really need is bread.

'Have you found Perry yet?'

I stop mid-air, my fork hovering in my hand. 'Is he here?'

'I don't know, I've never met him.' She laughs and the laugh turns into a snort which is of course what she's been doing. I hope she cleared it up and Mum doesn't get high when she cleans the loo tomorrow.

I feel inclined to stab her with my fork, but I suspect she wouldn't feel it.

I leave her cackling to herself and wander around the room. I smile over at Mum and Dad who are standing by the sink, alone and bewildered in their own home. I can tell by the look on Mum's face that she wants everyone to leave now. It's only a matter of time before she instructs me and my brothers' wives to start clearing the food away and collecting the glasses.

'Okay?' Henry says, when I bump into him. He smiles over at his wife, Jen. 'Mum and Dad have had enough, they're done in. Jen and Grace are going to start clearing the food in a minute, I'll be collecting the glasses.'

The wives are so well trained, so familiar with my mum's nuances, that they don't even need to be told.

☯☯☯

Gray drives us home. We've sneaked off before all the clearing up is finished, before the glasses are washed and put back into the boxes ready to be picked up, before the plates go into the dishwasher, before the leftovers go into the binbags. We've sneaked off before I have a meltdown. I never did find that bread to soak up the wine, so I just drank more instead.

'That went well,' Gray says.

Is he serious?

'What did?'

'The day.' He glances over at me, his knuckles turning white as he grips the steering wheel. At least he knows he's said the wrong thing. 'All things considered. As much as these days go.' He's backpedalling now. Too late.

Shall I let him off? Let it go?

'Mmm.' I turn away and look out of the window. I'm staring at nothing, nothing at all. I can't focus. Maybe Gray and I should end now. Today.

When we get home he helps me inside as though I am a frail old person. I shrug off my coat and he immediately whips it away, hangs it up with his own. Since Adam's death Gray has spent so much time here that he's almost moved in. It was a stealth move on his part that I hardly noticed. But it's been convenient, someone to hold me when it all gets too much. He has a few items of clothing and some toiletries here. The other day I caught him – is that the right phrase – loading the washing machine with our combined clothing. It seemed odd, almost obscene to think of his clothes mingling in soapy water with mine. But then, he has been sleeping in my bed. And more.

He's only recently moved back to the UK, lived in Dubai, or was it Abu Dhabi? I don't know. When I first met him in person he had quite the tan, but it's already faded since he's been back here in the gloomy UK. He jokes he's grown a beard because it's so cold.

He's renting a house but looking to buy one soon, he says.

I haven't given him a key to my flat though. It's far too soon for that.

'You sit down, I'll make a pot of tea,' he says, escorting me to the sofa. 'Did you eat anything? Would you like a sandwich?'

I nod without enthusiasm. Who knows, I might even eat it.

He disappears off into my kitchen, he hardly makes a sound, I'm grateful he's not a clatterer.

He brings back a cheese and pickle sandwich made with bread he brought from the nearby artisan baker shop yesterday. When we first met Gray would turn up with pastries and coffee, fresh rolls, even a cake once when he said we were celebrating our *one month since meeting online* anniversary. I remember the pleasure it brought when he did that.

'I could still take time off work and come on Monday,' he says, breaking into my thoughts.

'What?' Momentarily, I'm confused.

'I could come with you. To Adam's.'

'No, thanks. I need to do this on my own.' Now, don't mention it again.

I'm conflicted, grateful he's here, wishing he wasn't.

Three

6 months earlier

ADAM

You'd think I'd be able to find my one, wouldn't you? You know, my one true love, the one I'd die for.

I'm passable looking, no, I'm being modest, I'm better than passable, really quite attractive. I know that without anyone telling me, although I have been told on many occasions. Now I sound vain. Perhaps I am. Perhaps that's the problem.

I'm rich and famous, no modesty there you'll notice, because it's the truth. Adam Hames RA. The RA means I'm a Royal Academician which basically means I'm famous in the art world. Maybe that's what puts people off, maybe I should drop the RA.

I'm the perfect age, thirty-five. I move in the right circles, meet the kind of people I am attracted to, but nothing, zilch, nada.

Unless you count Jasper.

I don't count Jasper.

Don't misunderstand me, I adore Jasper. Always have, always will. He's my business manager and together we've done very well for each other. But he's pushing sixty and, despite the regular facials and beauty treatments, he looks it. I look up to Jasper in the same way I look up to my father. Jasper, however would welcome me into his bed any time. He told me so when we were first introduced – by my school art teacher no less – and in unguarded moments, when he's imbibed a little too much, he's told me so again since then. Recently.

Perhaps Jasper is my one.

No.

The doorbell rings, insistent, nonstop. It can be only one person.

I open the door and Angie flings herself at me. Sometimes I wish the concierge wouldn't let her in unannounced, but she's well known here. Martin, our permanent concierge will always buzz her in because he knows her, who she is to me. My sister.

'It ages since I last saw you,' she says, thumping me on the arm as though I've done something wrong.

'It's a mere three weeks. Don't be so melodramatic.'

She thumps me again, then drops her bag on the floor. I pick it up and carry it into what has become, over the years, her bedroom.

As I leave she wanders over to the glass bifold doors that lead out onto my balcony terrace that overlooks the Thames. She's still there when I return.

'That river never bores me,' she says, sighing. 'You have such a good view from up here. Such a contrast to my view of the back of *B&Q*. I can watch the delivery lorries any time I like.'

'You knew that when you bought your flat.' I'm not indulging her whinging.

'I did, but it was all I could afford.'

‘Sell the painting if you want to trade up.’

‘But then I won’t have it.’ She makes a face, poochy poo face we used to call it as children, puckering her lips, bending them down and frowning.

‘I’ll paint you another. Sell it.’

‘I couldn’t.’ Poochy poo again. ‘Though I might have to just to make ends meet.’

‘How’s work?’ I ask, which is not actually changing the subject but more diverting her. Over the years I’ve given her money, plenty, and I’ll happily do it again, but since she’s slightly older than me, I think perhaps she needs to stand on her own two feet. She’s never been good at that; I don’t know why.

‘There’s talk of redundancies.’

‘You’ll get a pay out if it happens to you.’

‘Not much. I haven’t been there long enough.’

‘You’ll get something else. Something better.’ I always say this; she’s had so many jobs.

She doesn’t answer, just looks off into the distance, back out onto the river. I think she regrets not taking a job with Dad and the brothers, but pride won’t let her ask them now.

‘Coffee? Tea? Something stronger?’

‘Tea, I think. Haven’t had tea in ages.’ She grins at me before pressing her nose against the glass. I’ll have to point that smudge out to the cleaners next week.

‘You had tea the last time you came. I remember I made a pot and you didn’t finish it.’

‘Like I said, ages. And don’t make a pot big enough for six, a teabag in a mug will do.’

I make my customary face to display my disgust before we both break into fits of laughter. Our mother would be horrified at the bag in a mug suggestion. We, you see, were brought up properly.

'How's Ma and Pa?'

'Same as. They asked when you'd be coming down to visit them.'

'It's not Mother's Day already, is it? Or have I missed it? You should have reminded me.'

'I'm not your wife,' she says, laughing. 'And, no, you haven't missed it.'

'It's their turn to come here, I visited them last.'

'That was Christmas, it doesn't count.'

'Bloody does.'

She shrugs and laughs and holds out her hands for the mug I'm now offering her. 'Did you put sugar in it?'

'No, darling, you're sweet enough already. How are the brothers and their crews?'

'Yeah, good. I think I will put sugar in it.' She marches towards the kitchen end of my open plan living area.

'This place is so immense, I'd quite forgotten.'

'Stop it.'

'What have you got planned for this weekend?' she asks, plonking herself down on one of my sofas.

I sit down next to her.

'Nothing much. Maybe we could order some food in, watch a bit of *Netflix*, catch up on the gossip.'

'Urgh. I can do that at home. I want excitement. Can't we go to a club?'

I groan. 'I'm exhausted after my travels. I just want to chill out at home. Spend time alone with you.' Now I do poochy poo face.

'Urgh, don't do that face, it makes you look ugly.'

'Yet it compliments you.'

She thumps me, and this time I suspect I probably deserve it.

'I'm tired. Jasper wore me out.'

She raises her eyebrows at me, grins.

'Not like that. Oh no. Not that he wouldn't. But I wouldn't.'

'No, be like sleeping with Dad.'

We both grimace.

'How *was* Germany?' she asks.

'Cold. Berlin is damn cold in March, not that it's much warmer here. Good though. Successful. Good show in the gallery. Sold a lot.'

'Good because you were away long enough.' She sounds so petulant.

'Well, I'm back now and have nothing planned for weekends for the foreseeable, so you can come every weekend if you want.'

'Maybe. I'll see how I'm fixed.' She grins again. 'Now I look at you properly, you do look tired.'

'Thanks.'

'So, okay, I'll let you off, no clubbing. *Netflix* and order in, but I want something decent, something expensive and lovely from one of your favourite restaurants.'

'Okay. I'm sure Carlo's will oblige, especially if we order before their rush.'

'What about lunch?' she asks.

'Lunch? We were talking about supper, early supper. Do we really need lunch?'

'I do,' she says before poking my stomach. 'Maybe you can go without.'

I suck my middle in and my cheeks before she laughs. I can't help joining in. 'Okay,' I say, 'let's go and get a cheese toasty down the café.'

She smiles sweetly at me, then allows the smile to turn into a big grin. 'I love that place.'

'Me too. It's a bit early though.'

'Not for me, I'm starving.'

'No breakfast?'

'Early train to catch.'

'Not that early,' I say, imagining her leaping out of bed and rushing out without a second thought for food.

The café is less than a five-minute walk from my place, it's a proper café, only open during the day, closes at five-thirty on the dot. The menu is basic and limited but delicious and filling. Proper comfort food. We find a seat inside because it's too cold to sit on the terrace overlooking the river; only the diehard smokers do that at this time of year.

'How's your love life?' Angie asks, biting into a toasted teacake, the butter oozing down her chin. She grabs a paper napkin and dabs at it.

I roll my eyes. 'How's yours?'

She also rolls her eyes. Then we giggle together.

'We're sad,' she says. 'Especially you. You have so much to offer.'

'And you don't?' She's a looker, my sister. Little and dark-haired, with a cheeky, elfin face. She has no problem attracting men, keeping them is another issue. Though it's usually her who does the dumping.

'Yes, but I've had a few boyfriends, you haven't. I was with Ewan for two years, on and off.'

'How is he? Do you ever see him?' She finished with Ewan when he asked her not to visit me so often, saying he thought her weekends should be spent with him. She'd never once invited him to come, even though I had.

'Married, with a baby.' She takes another bite of her teacake and more butter oozes.

'Ah.'

'It's what he always wanted.'

'With you?'

'With anybody. I must have been his type though, because his wife looks just like me. There but for the grace of God…'

'What a dysfunctional pair we are. Look at the brothers, all happily settled many moons ago, lovely wives, lovely children.'

'You'd never have a lovely wife, would you?' She looks at me pointedly. 'You're gay.'

I sigh and shake my head. 'You're not, what's your excuse… for not having a family I mean?'

She shrugs before looking off into the distance, apparently deep in thought.

'We're going to find you someone to love,' she announces, stuffing the last bit of teacake into her mouth.

'Just like that.'

'Yep, just like that. Come on, hurry up, I need a walk now before it gets any colder, looks like it might rain.'

☯☯☯

Carlo's doesn't really do takeaways or deliveries, but I'm a good customer and friendly with Carlo so he sends something delicious our way. It arrives just after six, that was the compromise, but since we haven't eaten anything since noon, we're both ravenous. We have the food arranged, still in its containers, on the coffee table and we're lounging on the sofa.

'This is so good,' Angie says, while stuffing more into her mouth.

'Okay, no need to rush, there's plenty.'

'I know, I'm just hungry. Anyway…' She narrows her eyes at me. '…are you suggesting I'm getting fat?'

'Fat? You. As though that's likely. I'm the one running

to fat. Jasper told me all queers end up fat.'

Angie's mouth drops open, I lean over and close it with my fingertip mostly because there's still food in there and it's not a pretty sight.

'He shouldn't even think things like that, never mind say them.'

I laugh, just as I did when he said it.

'I told him that, he says he can say what he likes about queers because he is one.'

Angie shakes her head in what I interpret as disbelief and horror. 'I suppose it's his age,' she says.

Now my mouth drops open. 'That's ageist. Now who's prejudiced?'

Her response is to grab another forkful of food and ram it into her mouth. 'Anyway, you're not fat.' She eyes my stomach. 'Maybe not as toned as you were.'

'That's enough fat talk.'

I have put on a few pounds, especially after spending time in Berlin with Jasper. We ate far too much and far too often. Angie, conversely, looks thinner than ever. She is so different to the rest of my family, my parents, me, my brothers, we're all tall where Angie is tiny. She's dark haired too, where we are all fair, though in the case of my older brothers, thinning – I suppose I have that to look forward to.

When we were teenagers I used to tease Angie about her looks. Not that she wasn't, isn't, beautiful, she's quite a head turner, just that she didn't match the rest of us. Then our mother produced a yellowing photo of her own grandmother and there she was, Angie's double. For a while I teased her about being reincarnated.

'Hey,' she says, 'have you got any kitchen roll? I'm afraid I'm going to drop some of this on my clothes. This sauce looks like it won't wash out.'

‘Sorry, yes. We should have eaten at the table and laid it out properly.’ I get up, pad across the room, open a drawer and pull out two linen napkins. Just as I’m about to close the drawer I see it, a black stone in the shape of yin, or is it yang? I can never remember which is which. I came across it a few months ago deep in a trunk among some old paints, don’t know what it was doing there. I popped it in this drawer waiting for Angie to visit, then forgot about it. Angie has its matching twin.

I remember the summer we found those stones on a beach in Greece, we must have been ten. August, that one month of the year when we are the same age. Mum said they must have been manmade because they couldn’t possibly be so near perfect and fit together so well. A pair of commas, one black, one white, forming the perfect circle. We pestered Dad to drill holes in them, ‘the eyes’ Angie had said, but he wouldn’t, said it would ruin them. Mum stuck googly eyes on them instead. I don’t know where they came from. The memory brings a smile to my face. Such a long time ago.

‘Should definitely have sat at the table,’ I say, flinging a napkin at her as I sit back down on the sofa.

She snatches at it and tuts.

I lay the stone on the table and wait for her to notice.

‘Hey, what’s that?’ She grabs the stone as I grin. ‘It’s yin.’ She holds the stone to her heart. ‘I’d forgotten all about these. It’s still got its eye. How I’ve missed you, yin.’

‘Bit melodramatic. Do you still have yang?’

She stares at me for a moment or two. ‘Must have, I’ve never binned it. I’ll have to search it out now.’ She strokes my stone. ‘It’s so smooth, so shiny.’

‘All that rubbing,’ I say and we both burst into laughter.

'Life was a lot simpler then, wasn't it?'

'Of course it was, we were kids.' I nudge her and she laughs again.

'You know,' she says, turning serious on me, 'the only way to get Jasper off your case is to get yourself a boyfriend.'

'Well, yes, I think so.' I roll my eyes and she laughs again.

'After dinner we're going online and we're going to investigate a few dating apps. Find you someone lovely.'

'I don't think so.'

'Oh yes.' She grins again and nods her head slowly.

'Hunt for yourself too.'

'Been there, done that. But you haven't.'

'And I don't intend to.'

Four

'Jasper thinks it's a terrible idea,' I tell Angie when she arrives the following weekend. 'Says I could be letting myself in for all sorts of trouble.'

'Of course he says that, because he wants you for himself.' She holds her bag out for me to take to her room, which of course I do.

When I come back she's making us both a coffee from my machine and she's already put the biscuit tin on the coffee table. After she takes our coffees over, she plonks herself down on the sofa and holds out her hand.

'What?'

'Phone. I want a status update and from the few messages and that short phone call we had in the week I know I can't rely on you to give me the full story.' She grins.

She always grins and it's so disarming. It always has been. I suspect her grin, even though she was a baby herself when I was born, was the first thing that imprinted itself onto my brain. I've always felt closer to Angie than our mother. Not that I blame our dear ma, she had more than her hands full before I bounced into the world, the baby that should never have been.

'Well?' she says, still holding out her hand.

Reluctantly, and with a lot of fake sighing and eyerolling, I hand over my phone.

'How many have you swiped?' she asks, as she grabs my phone. I don't even need to give her the password because she knows it. There's very little about me that she doesn't know. 'And, more importantly, how many have you matched with?'

I grin as I shake my head. 'Oh no, you're the expert, see if you can work it out.'

It doesn't take her long. 'Three, you've swiped three. Is that it? Dozens have swiped for you.' Before I can answer she's flicking through my phone again. 'And you've matched with three. Good going, little bro.'

'Thanks.' I hold my hand out for my phone, but she clutches it to her chest.

'Seems that profile we worked on has done the trick.' What she means is the profile that *she* worked on, since I had very little to do with it. She even took a carefully posed photo of me, twisted my head into a most unnatural position to pick up the light and, in her words, hide the bags under my eyes. She had me do a sort of pout too. If I ever meet any of these men in real life I'm going to have to contort my face and neck into a very unnatural pose before they will recognise me.

'Yes, all those words you wrote…' I laugh.

'All true, little brother.' We hadn't mentioned my fame, my career, or my richness, as she calls it. She said it would attract the wrong sort. Instead we focussed on my kindness, my humour, my charity work – which is stretching it a bit, since the only charity work I can claim is once a year I donate a painting to a different charity so they can sell it and use the funds. It was Jasper's idea years ago, and it's excellent PR, he ensures the charity publicise it for months. It's also excellent tax-wise apparently, but I leave that to my accountant.

'Can I have my phone back now please?'

'No, not yet. We need to examine these matches carefully.'

'I have. Thank you.' I hold my hand out again.

She shakes her head and frowns at me, but she doesn't offer the phone back, instead swiping it open, keying in my password again and bringing up the first match.

'He looks okay,' she says. 'Have you exchanged any messages with him?' She shows me his photo.

'Not yet.'

'This one?' she asks, after examining another one.

'No.'

'And finally, this one? Oh, hello. Reading between the lines it looks like he works in the creative industries too.'

'He does.'

'You talked to him?'

I nod.

'And?'

'We had an online chat, then spoke on the phone.' I'm not telling her that the phone call lasted hours and actually went on past midnight. Or that it was the first of many.

'And? What's he like? What does he do?'

'He's a photographer, he's in his late twenties and he sounds very nice.'

'Meeting in person?'

'Not yet.'

'Do you plan to?'

'I think so.' I'm being disingenuous, we're meeting for dinner on Sunday evening. I plan to drop Angie at Paddington Station then carry on to the restaurant. I'm driving to prevent me from drinking myself stupid.

'Does he know who you are?'

'Not specifically. I've told him I'm an artist. I might have alluded to greetings cards and stuff.'

'Mmm.'

'What?'

'Well, I suppose it is the truth, albeit an old truth.'

'You were the one who told me not to let on about who I was or I'd be pursued by gold diggers.'

She tosses my phone back at me and I just catch it before it hits the floor, which wouldn't be a good thing for the phone since my floors are terrazzo and somewhat hard.

'Okay, I want a full breakdown when you do meet him. When is that again?'

'Tomo…' Damn it.

'Caught you. I knew you were lying. Little liar Adam.'

'Shut up. Did you want to go out tonight?'

'Yes. Of course I do.'

☯☯☯

The date went okay but there was no chemistry between us. Funny, given how long we'd chatted on the phone, but in person, nothing, nada, zilch. I was disappointed but pragmatic, Angie, however was heartbroken on my behalf.

Before I'd dropped her off at the station we'd agreed that she would ring me an hour into the date, this coincided with the end of her journey, so she'd just have got off the train by then. If it was going well I'd keep the call very brief, if not, I'd tell my date there was an emergency and I needed to leave.

As it turned out, it didn't matter either way. It was going okay but once we'd eaten, my date – he said his name was Paul – decided that there was no future for us and left. Fortunately he didn't leave me to pay the bill, but left his half on the table. It was all rather distasteful and I have no intention of repeating the experience ever again.

'You can't let one shitty date spoil everything,' Angie says the following weekend.

'Nah, it was a dumb idea anyway. Who needs a man? I don't. I'm successful, talented, rich…'

'Course you are, but everyone deserves to love and be loved in return.'

'What about you?' I ask, as much to shift the focus away from me.

'What about me?'

'Where's your lover?'

She groans. 'Been there, done that, several times. Don't know if I have the energy to get to know someone new again. But you don't have that excuse, you need to dive in and have another go. Phone,' she demands, holding out her hand.

We spend the rest of the weekend swiping until we have a few more matches for me. By the time Angie goes home, I have contacted my original matches plus two new ones.

It's going to be a busy time for me. Maybe.

But, as it turned out, nothing came of any of them.

☯☯☯

'You can't just give up,' Angie says over lunch one Saturday. We're in one of my favourite restaurants; the food is good, the service excellent.

'To be honest, Angie, it's all sapped my strength, tried my patience and Jasper says it's definitely affected my work. I'm done with it. If you want to matchmake, do it on yourself.'

'Jasper would say that, wouldn't he?' She makes the poochy poo face.

If we weren't in public I'd reach over and slap her one.

'Right,' I say, sounding decisive. 'That topic is not for further discussion. Have you chosen yet?' I don't want to fall out with my sister over something so intangible. My not having a boyfriend really isn't an issue, any more than her not having one. And it's nothing new.

'Shame we're related,' she says, grinning. 'Because I think we'd make the perfect couple, you so rich, me so charming.'

I stare at her. Sometimes I do wonder what goes on in her head. 'Apart from the incest and you not being a man, I think that's an excellent idea.' I can't keep the sarcasm from my voice. 'We don't need to be a couple, we're siblings. Believe me, from my perspective, that's more than enough.'

And that was that. We didn't discuss it again. Although I didn't delete the app from my phone and I kept my profile live, and despite not swiping any I liked, I did look again occasionally.

☯☯☯

Another month passed and I didn't give the dating scene any more thought. I was deeply into my work, totally preoccupied with an upcoming gallery exhibition that Jasper had pulled out of the bag at short notice. He was on my case constantly, checking I was putting in the hours and inspecting what I produced. Don't ever let anyone tell you that being an artist is about art, it isn't, it's about production, or at least it is with Jasper on your back. But it's finished now, everything has gone to the gallery.

'I'm taking you out to lunch,' Jasper declares. Having let himself into my place unannounced, he's crept into my studio and caught me sketching out my next piece.

'What the f…' I yell, my voice high pitched and sounding very like a girl's.

Jasper just laughs in response.

'I need to have a word with the concierge downstairs and take that key off you.'

'Never, darling,' he says, with a grin. 'This place is a bit scrappy; do you want a hand tidying it up?'

I glance over at him, he's dressed in a pale cream linen suit, with some sort of peachy, silk blouse affair underneath it. He couldn't look any more foppish and camp if he tried. He spins around my studio, stepping over paint-covered rags on the floor and fake shuddering when he knocks into an easel. Yes, it is a mess, but I've been working flat out for weeks. This show he's put together has stressed me out, conversely working under such pressure has spurred me on to produce some of my finest works.

'You're hardly dressed for housework, are you?' I make a show of looking him up and down.

He laughs. 'Not me, darling, not me. I've got an intern type, who would just love to work with you… clearing up and such.'

'No thanks. I hope you're paying the intern.'

He scowls at me. 'Of course. Anyway, leave all this detritus behind now, we're off to lunch. Have you showered today?'

'Detritus? Cheeky sod.'

An hour later and we're sitting in Bib and Tucker; recently opened and just a few minutes' walk from my place. It's Jasper's latest favourite restaurant which he assures me is where he takes all his best clients. I'm his best client and it's the first time he's taken me. I'm surprised Angie hasn't spotted this place though.

'All the paintings arrived at the gallery yesterday,' he says, as though it's news to me.

'I know, I was there when they left my studio.'

'Excellent. Gerard, the gallery manager, rang me this morning positively hysterical with excitement.'

'Good. There are some good pieces there.'

'Indeed there are. Shall we have wine? I think we've earned it.' He snatches up the wine list.

I certainly feel as though I have. I'm quite exhausted and am definitely in need of a little rest and recouperation. Who knows, I might even revisit that dating app.

As if reading my mind – how could he possibly – Jasper suddenly says, 'How's the dating going?'

I wave my hand at him as dismissively as I can. 'I've hardly had time for that, have I? I even had to stop my sister from coming up the last few weekends. She's not very happy with me.'

'Ah, the delectable Angie, how is she?'

'Sulking, if you must know. She misses her London weekends.'

'Invite her to the opening,' he says, as though it's his decision whether she can come or not.

'Well, thank you. I just might.'

We have a pleasant meal and talk about nothing much. To be honest I'm so exhausted I'd have been quite happy just to veg out at home or, more productively, have a damn good tidy up of my studio.

Jasper, always known for his dramatic arm waving is wittering on about someone I absolutely must meet – not romantically he adds, rather cryptically – when I catch the eye of a guy watching him. And smiling.

He's probably my age, maybe older, has the blondest hair I've ever seen, which makes me think of a Viking, but his eyes are so dark that they shock me. Maybe it's the light in here. I study his profile, his jawline. I'd love to paint him. When Jasper gets up to go to the toilet, the guy saunters over and stops at our table.

'Hello,' he says, and waits for me to answer.

'Err, hi. Do I know you?' I am somewhat used to people approaching me because I am a bit famous, but it usually follows a piece in one of the papers or weekend supplements. Nothing like that has happened lately.

'No, you don't. You just caught my eye.' He winks.

'Right.' It's ridiculous but I feel myself blushing under his gaze.

He presses a business card onto the table, smiles again, then turns to walk away. 'Call me if you feel so inclined.'

Then he leaves, sauntering out without a backward glance, just as Jasper drops back into his seat. I snatch up the business card and drop it into my jacket pocket.

Five

'It's so good to be here again.' Angie throws her arms about and twirls out onto the balcony. It's a warm spring day so I have the doors pulled as far back as they can go.

'Always so melodramatic.'

'Yes, but I've missed you. What are we doing today?'

'Ice skating.'

'What?'

'I've booked us a lesson.'

'You're joking, right?'

I laugh, but I'm not joking.

An hour later and we're lacing up skate boots and listening to a list of dos and don'ts from the instructor.

'Your face is as white as the ice,' I whisper, nudging my sister.

'We could be sitting out in the sunshine, having lunch. Why are we doing this?'

'I just fancied it. I thought it would cool us off. I thought it might cut down all the wine we slosh back. Do something different.' I arch my eyebrows at her and she scowls back. 'We can go for a late lunch after this.'

'I should think so too.'

We stumble onto the ice, give our best, or at least I do; I'm not entirely sure Angie does. When the lesson is over, the relief on Angie's face is obvious. She's only fallen over twice more than me, so she hasn't done so badly.

'I enjoyed that,' I say, grinning.

'I hated it. Don't ever book us, me, in for more.'

'Oh, but it's a course, six lessons over six weeks.'

'No way.' She shakes her head as she yanks at the laces on the skate boots. Not waiting for me, she stomps over to retrieve her shoes, then slips them on without coming back for me.

It takes me a lot longer to retrieve my shoes and put them on.

'I don't know what you were thinking. I hated that as a kid.' Her mouth is set in a straight line of annoyance as I catch up with her. She's leaning against the rail watching the skating.

'I enjoyed it today. I never did it as a kid.'

'You did.'

'I didn't,' I insist.

'You haven't really bought six lessons, have you?'

I grin.

'You bastard.' She thumps me on the arm.

'Hey, that's my painting arm.'

'Good.'

We're just turning to leave when I'm sure I catch sight of a very blond-headed man twirling around on the ice like a pro. Was it him, I wonder? I lose sight of him again; the rink is so crowded. I remember the business card still sitting in the desk drawer in my studio. Will I ring him?

'You owe me the best lunch ever for subjecting me to that.'

'Seriously,' I say. 'I think I might book the full course, that was just a taster.'

'Don't book it on the weekend because I won't be

coming.'

'I'll see what's available,' I say, thinking about the blond man again. Does he come here every Saturday? Was it actually him? 'You do know that I have to work during the week, just like you.'

She gives me a withering look. 'You're self-employed,' she says. 'You can please yourself.'

Sunday evening and I've just got back from dropping Angie at the station when I wander into my studio. I say wander, but it's not aimless, I know exactly what I'm doing. I fish the card out of the drawer and, without giving myself a chance to think about it, I ring him.

It's a mobile number and it goes straight to voicemail. I feel unreasonably disappointed.

'Perry Oblekt, leave your name and number,' his voice is professional, efficient.

I don't know what to say, so end the call, then chide myself for it because he told me to ring him. Damn it.

I study his card further, his name is odd, certainly that surname, definitely a Viking name, I decide. I flick the card back into my drawer.

An hour later and my phone rings, the number looks familiar.

'Hello?'

'Hey, hi, Perry Oblekt here, you rang me?' The inflection in his voice goes up at the end of the sentence. He sounds less sure of himself than I would have expected. Certainly less confident than in the restaurant.

'Hi, yeah. You left your card with me in Bib and Tucker the other day.'

There's a pause, not long, but long enough to make

me wish I hadn't answered the phone, hadn't made the call in the first place.

'Ah, of course, you were with the flamboyant guy.'

I suppress a snort. Jasper would just love being described as flamboyant. 'That's right, I was.'

'Hey, how are you?'

'Good, good.' Now what do I say?

'Me too, me too. Would you like to snatch a drink sometime?'

Snatch a drink, I almost laugh. 'Yes, sure.'

'Just need to check my diary.' I can hear pages turning, he is literally checking his diary. 'What about Friday evening?'

'Yes, I can do that.'

We agree a place and time and after the call has ended I find myself excited, elated, nervous. I'm assuming he's gay, I'm assuming he knows I am. I don't think I'm overtly so like Jasper but the signs must be there. I'm not used to men approaching me like that, it's only ever happened twice and one of those times was in a gay bar. But then, I've never approached anyone myself either.

I don't tell Angie about my date, if it is a date. I should, but I'm going to wait and see how it pans out. It may be that Perry Oblekt recognised me and wants to… wants to what? Sell my paintings, oust Jasper. He could be an agent; he could easily not be gay.

My phone pings. I grab it, aware that my heart is suddenly beating faster. I hope it's not a dick pic.

It is a photo but it's from Angie.

Hey, look what I found. Matching pair. It's a picture of her yang stone, smooth and white. *I'll bring it up with me at the weekend. No eye though.* ☹ *Don't book any skating.*

I assure her I won't.

My gallery opening night is Thursday. I'm all dressed up and listening to Jasper assure me that everything will be sold in the first few days. I hope he's right. Despite my success I still get nervous about my paintings selling. He's all over the gallery owner too, a man who is very much like Jasper in style and mannerisms.

'Gerard and I went to school together,' Jasper informs me, which explains a lot.

'Time to open those doors, gents. Everybody ready?' Gerard nods around the waiters who are standing by with trays of drinks before heading for the front door. 'I hope you've invited all your friends and family.' He turns and grins at me as the first few people saunter in.

I did invite my family, but the notice was short and no one could make it, not even Angie. She's quite cross with me for not letting her know earlier which I admit was rather remiss of me, I wanted her to come. She said she can't take any more time off work until the start of the new holiday year, whatever that means. She said I don't understand these things; she's right, I don't. She said I'm rich and privileged. I reminded her that I've earned my money and my privilege.

I wonder if I should have invited Perry Oblekt?

No, too soon.

The evening is a success. Jasper and Gerard are twin grinning. Observing them from a distance, their heads together, their reflective body language, it occurs to me that they would make a great couple. Jasper sees me staring and heads towards me.

'Adam, darling boy, such a great evening. You've made us both very happy.'

I'm not sure if he means me and him or him and

Gerard.

Gerard sees the last guest out, locks the doors and comes over to join us. He's still grinning.

'I'm so glad Jasper persuaded me to host you. I'll be honest, I had my doubts, not sure if my clientele would like some of your modernist pieces, but…' He lets the words hang there.

Modernist pieces, no one has ever said that about my work before.

Behind Gerard's back Jasper performs a theatrical eye roll. I just nod and smile.

'Now I do expect you to pop in every day even if you only hang about for an hour or so, so that the punters can see you.' So they're punters now. 'And bring your own guests too.'

'I'll do my best,' I assure him. But it's highly likely the only guest I will bring will be Angie and she's not going to buy anything. She only has one of my paintings because I gave it to her. Unless she's already sold it.

☯☯☯

Friday evening finds me brimming with excitement and fear. I've told no one, not Angie, not Jasper.

What if he's a weirdo?

What if he thinks I am?

I dress carefully, smart, young professional with a twist. Who am I kidding? I opt for jeans that are clean and smart and roomy enough around the waist that if we eat – we haven't said we will but I've not eaten this evening just in case – I won't be bulging over the top of them.

I turn up at the pub, his suggestion. A place I've never been to, it's one of those proper old London boozers, tucked away in a side street, dark wood panelling and the odd bit of stained glass. It's small too. I scan the place looking for his distinctive blond hair. I'm not early but bang on time and so should he be.

He's stood me up.

Great.

I head for the bar, mainly because the barman is looking at me expectantly, valuing every customer since there are so few in here. I'll look a fool if I turn around and march out; conversely, I feel a fool for staying.

I order beer because that's what real men drink, don't they?

I'm just taking a sip from the pint when a voice speaks from behind me.

'Hey,' it says.

I turn. It's him. Smiling, his eyes twinkling. He leans over towards the barman and says, 'I'll have what he's having.' Then he turns back to me and holds out his hand. 'Perry Oblekt,' he says. His grip is warm and firm, soft, comforting.

That's when I realise he doesn't actually know me. We've never been introduced; I've never told him my name. I suppose it's possible he recognises me, but I doubt it. 'I'm Adam,' I say. 'Pleased to meet you.'

'Adam.' He lets my name linger on his lips. 'No surname yet?' He smirks.

'Sorry, Hames.' Of course I don't add RA. That would be a pompous step too far.

'Well, Mr Hames, it's nice to meet you. Shall we sit over there?' He points to a corner table but his eyes flick towards the barman who seems inordinately interested in our exchange.

After we sit down we both sup our pints before putting them back down on the table. The barman saunters over and drops a couple of beermats down for us.

'Thanks,' we say, both lifting our pints onto the mats.

Perry rolls his eyes and shakes his head slightly. Momentarily it reminds me of Jasper.

Now I'm here I don't know what to say and, judging by the silence, neither does Perry, although he isn't averse to running his eyes over my face and body. The silence and his scrutiny are unnerving.

'That guy you were with at the restaurant, is that your father?'

I laugh. 'No. No. My business associate.'

'Cool.' He leans across the table, his voice almost a whisper and I can feel his breath on my skin. 'I was worried he might be your lover, your sugar daddy.'

Ah, so we are on the same page. I shake my head.

'I take it you have no significant other?' He arches his eyebrows.

'No.'

'Nor me.' He smiles again, twinkles his eyes. He really is most attractive 'Just like to get things straight. I don't like messy relationships.'

I don't know what to say.

'So, Adam, tell me about yourself.'

I gabble on about my family, Angie specifically, telling him how she visits every weekend. I tell a few anecdotes about our childhood before finally saying, 'Your turn.'

A slow smile spreads across his face. Then he begins to tell me all about himself.

Six

I've decided to tell Angie about Perry. It's only fair, she's always confided in me about her relationships, no matter how disastrous.

She'll be pleased for me. It was, after all, her idea that I should get on the dating train, albeit via dating apps. Although that didn't pan out as well as the old-fashioned way has.

'You've what?' she says, five minutes after she's burst through the door on Saturday morning. 'You've been on a date and you didn't tell me beforehand? Which one was it? Let me see your phone.'

'I didn't meet him online. Our meeting was pure chance.' I tell her about the restaurant, about the business card.

'Well, aren't you the lucky one. And isn't he. What's he like?'

'He's blond, his hair is shoulder length I'd say.' In my head I'm remembering his hair as it brushed against his jacket. 'He's half Swedish. Got a bit of a Viking vibe about him.'

'Sounds a bit elvish,' she says, giggling. She means from *Lord of the Rings*.'

I think about that for a little too long, remembering

how we both had a crush on *Legolas* as played by Orlando Bloom, his long blond hair so straight and smooth and how disappointed we were when we found out the actor was dark-haired in real life.

'Not really,' I say. 'Definitely more Viking.'

'Is he big?' She pulls her little arms up and makes muscles.

'Not especially.' I gently pull her arms down before changing the subject. 'What would you like to do today?'

'Not ice skating.'

'No?'

She narrows her eyes. 'No, and you'd better not have booked me in for more.'

'I haven't.' What I'm not telling her is that Perry has suggested he gives me a few impromptu lessons. He told me that the rink is available for a freestyle session immediately after the lesson session, that it *was* him I saw on the rink as we left. That he often goes and thoroughly enjoys it. He learnt to skate as a kid when visiting his grandparents in Sweden. He wanted me to come today, but I've told him I can't because of Angie. *He* can't do a week day due to work pressures.

'Tell me more about him,' my sister says, breaking into my thoughts.

'Who?'

'This man you're seeing. You haven't even told me his name.'

'Perry Oblekt.'

'That's a weird name.'

'I told you, he's Swedish, well, half.'

She grins.

Before she launches into it, I warn her off. 'Don't do the Swedish chef.'

'What? As if I would.'

I don't even smile at that; I just know she wanted to. 'He doesn't even speak like that, he was brought up here, though obviously he does speak Swedish.'

'What does he do?' she asks, wisely deciding to heed my warning.

'Imports and exports.'

'Drug dealer,' she says, leaning back and scrutinising me.

'He's not a bloody drug dealer. I'd forgotten how horrible you can be sometimes.'

'Just looking out for you, little bro.'

I hate that phrase, it's so demeaning on so many levels, not least because I'm twice her size. I don't need her looking out for me, it's much more the other way round.

'What does he import, or export?'

'I don't know.' I do. I'm lying. He told me all about it last night. He told me that vintage Swedish furniture is *de rigueur* in London at the moment. I know if I say this Angie will immediately make a quip about *IKEA*, and I have to admit it was the first thought that popped into my head when he mentioned it. 'Coffee or tea?' I ask, getting up and heading towards the kitchen.

'Whatever you're having,' she says, pulling out her phone. When I come back with our mugs, she's studying her phone. 'I've googled him. Can't find him anywhere. How do you spell that surname? It's a weird one, isn't it?'

I spell it out. 'He doesn't have social media accounts under his own name, everything's under his company name.'

'Which is?' She waves her phone at me before grabbing her coffee.

It would be easy not to tell her, or tell her to mind her own business, but, on the other hand, why not? She is, after all, my sister and definitely looking out for me, however unnecessary. I tell her the company's name and she googles it before spending a lot of time flicking through the pages.

'Wow, have you seen the price of some of this stuff?'

I shrug. 'It's very popular.'

'Look at this.' She thrusts her phone at me and shows me a cast iron and wooden garden bench that looks as though it has seen better times. 'Mum and Dad had one like that, do you remember?' Without waiting for a reply and pulling back her phone, she continues. 'The wood rotted and Dad burnt it one Bonfire Night. I think he still has the iron ends hanging up in the garage. I might send him this and tell him to fish them out.' She laughs, I don't. 'Oh look, they allow others to sell stuff on their website.'

'Yes.' Perry had told me how to meet demand he had allowed third party sellers to participate, for a commission, obviously.

'Found him,' she says. 'Per Oblekt. Ah, no pic though. That's a shame. Do you have one?'

'No. I didn't take a picture on our date, why would I do that? I've only just met the guy.' And I wasn't even sure it was a date.

'Next time then.'

'Maybe.'

'When can I meet him?'

'Not yet. Early days and all that.' I smile at her, she's sweet really, and just interested yet I find her questions intrusive.

'Look at the price of this,' she screeches. 'Seven hundred pounds for an old chair, it's not even nice.' She waves her phone past my face.

'I think it's rather nice.'

'Would you pay that for some old tat? Really?'

I shake my head and pick up our empty mugs.

'You London types,' she says, shaking her head. 'No one at home would pay that.'

'I'm not a London type.'

'Course you are. He must be absolutely loaded.' She laughs.

I change the subject. 'I need to show my face at the gallery. You'll enjoy that. You haven't seen my new show.'

'What about lunch?'

'I can make you a quick sandwich if you're hungry. We'll go for dinner later.'

She makes a face and stuffs her phone back in her bag.

At the gallery Gerard is delighted to see us. He makes a big show of hugging first me then Angie even though he's never met her.

'I missed you yesterday,' he says.

'Yes, sorry, I got tied up.' I didn't, I just didn't feel like coming which is rather unprofessional of me.

'Well, not to worry, Jasper was here and did an excellent job talking you up and as a result sold two more.' Gerard's smile is so wide it must hurt.

'That's great, good old Jasper.'

'Less of the old, darling,' Gerard says, as Angie grins at me behind his back.

We spend a couple of hours at the gallery, me charming and smarming; Angie, after an initial whizz around my paintings, hiding in the tiny staff kitchen and playing with her phone. She can be quite immature sometimes.

During those couple of hours I check my phone too, often. I want Perry to message me like he said he would.

Or was that just a casual aside, a little bit of politeness to mask his true intention of never crossing paths with me again? I'm paranoid. I thought we got on so well, he said he'd take me skating. He kissed me lightly on the mouth before we parted. He said he'd message me in the morning. Morning has now well and truly passed.

'Can we go now?' Angie asks. She looks like a bored teenager.

☯☯☯

I really don't feel like going out. It's obvious that Perry isn't going to message; morning and afternoon have been and gone and we're now into evening. I feel a fool. I feel cheated. I've gone and told Angie about him and now he's ghosting me. What an idiot I am. This is why I've never been in a long-term relationship because people, that is lovers, aren't to be trusted.

'Ready?' Angie asks. 'Where are we going?'

I don't know and I don't care. 'Where would you like? You choose.' I force a smile.

'Oh, haven't you booked anywhere? Will we even get a table anywhere decent?'

'Don't be so dramatic,' I snap.

'Okay, okay. What's wrong with you? You were all jolly and sunny this morning.'

'Headache,' I mutter.

'Oh.'

I watch her deflate then sink onto the sofa. 'Does that mean you don't want to go out.' She's all dressed up with nowhere to go.

'No, let's go. I'm probably just hungry.' There's an element of truth in that because I haven't eaten anything since breakfast; I didn't bother making myself a sandwich when I made Angie one.

Her eyes light up, she jumps up and we're off. We easily get a table in Bib and Tucker around the corner – Angie's first visit and she's impressed. I admit that after eating, and drinking, I do feel a lot better, although I've rejected Angie's suggestion that we go clubbing.

We're on our way home, arm in arm, when she suddenly asks the question that my subconscious has been dreading all day.

'So, when are you seeing lover boy again? What's his name again?' As if she could forget after all that googling nonsense.

'I don't know if I will. We left it quite fluid. Not sure I want to get into all that messy business.'

'Eww,' she says, before cackling a little too loudly – she's had even more to drink than me. 'Too much detail…'

'I didn't mean that. I meant relationships, expectations, considerations…'

'Right.' She sighs. 'Why don't you just loosen up, little bro.'

☯☯☯

It's a relief when I finally drop Angie at the station on Sunday evening. She's been too perky, too aware this weekend and, unusually, I've found her annoying. We almost had a row when she asked about Perry again, then teased me for being needy when I finally relented and told her he hadn't messaged. She said that perhaps I'm not good boyfriend material if I'm going to be so sulky. I reminded her that I never wanted a boyfriend in the first place and that this had all been her idea. Her fault. Her retort was that she planned to vet anyone who matched with me and that meeting someone in real life, organically as she called it, had not been part of the plan.

Anyway, she's gone home now. Her parting shot was that she expects to meet Perry if I'm still friends with him next weekend. When she said 'friends with him' she did the poochy poo face. I love her but she can be so annoying at times.

On the way home I stop at the late-night minimart, go in and buy a family-sized packet of *Doritos* and a jar of salsa dip. When the shop assistant asks me if I need anything else I assume he means alcohol or cigarettes. But I have a bottle of red wine already waiting for me at home. And maybe, after that, if I can't sleep, I'll paint. I'm feeling the muse upon me, not something that happens often as after all these years I'm quite a disciplined artist.

I've finished the wine, the *Doritos* and the salsa and am lying back feeling sick, flicking through *Netflix* and knowing I won't be painting tonight, when my phone pings.

It could be him.

It's not, it's Angie. She's home, she always messages to tell me. And she's added a picture of yang, which has languished in her handbag all weekend without her showing it to me.

Next time, she writes.

Definitely.

I drop my phone on the sofa, lean back and close my eyes. I feel shit now. Binge eating and drinking is not a good idea.

My phone rings.

'Hey, it's Perry. Sorry it's so late.' It's 10pm.

'Yeah,' I say.

'Had a nightmare of a weekend.'

Seven

'What kind of nightmare?' I ask, thinking it had better be serious.

'My mum had a stroke.' That's all he says, then silence.

'Is she okay?'

'Well, kind of. They got her to hospital pretty sharpish but she's sedated and very ill. Don't know how it will affect her when she comes round. Been a bit touch and go.'

'I'm so sorry. When did it happen?'

'Saturday, early morning. That's where I've been all weekend, at the hospital.'

'You still there?'

'No, I've had to come back, got to fly out early tomorrow. Really didn't want to leave her but…' There's a catch in his voice and I hear him inhale deeply. 'Anyway, needs must. My aunt, Mum's sister, is stepping into the breach, so to speak. Sorry I didn't ring you as promised.'

'Oh no, that's fine, I fully understand. I'm so sorry,' I say again, feeling both guilty and selfish.

'Hey, yeah, because the last thing I'd want to do is ghost you. I thought we got on really well.'

'Me too,' I say, grinning to myself now, maybe it's the

wine.

'I really want to see you again.'

'Me too.'

'Look, I'm away all week, back Thursday, want to spend Friday and Sunday with my mum but we can still do that skating thing on Saturday morning. And if you're up for it I have tickets for that musical at the Adelphi on Saturday evening. Would you like to go?'

I think about Angie, about putting her off because obviously I don't want her coming on my date, my two dates. 'Umm,' I say, thinking slowly. 'My sister is due up at the weekend.'

'Ah, I see. Never mind, some other time. Hey, maybe you and her could use the theatre tickets.'

'We couldn't do that.'

'You might as well, I won't go on my own.' He laughs.

'Did you buy the tickets for us?' I'm quite taken aback.

'No, to be honest I was given them by a grateful client. I just thought it would be something you and I could enjoy together. But I understand if you've already got a date with your sister.'

A date with my sister. Put like that it sounds even sadder than it is. Before I can say anything he starts speaking again.

'I'm off again early the following Monday morning, only a couple of days but I want to spend some more time with my mum after that.'

'Of course.'

'Anyway, let me know about those tickets. I'd better go now, early start and all that.'

'No,' I say, not wanting him to end the call. 'I could put my sister off, it's not a firm arrangement for anything special. She comes up most weekends so a weekend off won't be a problem.' Even as I say it, I know that Angie will be annoyed.

'Well, if you're sure,' he says. 'I wouldn't want to come between a guy and his sister.'

'No, really, she'll understand.' Sort of.

☯☯☯

I break the news to Angie on Monday evening, she's not impressed, irritated that she's having to give up her London weekend, and annoyed that she's not getting to vet Perry first. She does the 'little bro' thing again, telling me to be careful and I remind her that I'm a big boy now. Really, you'd think she'd know that by now, I'm the one with the stellar career and swanky London penthouse. I don't say that, I don't need to and it would be extremely immature of me.

Saturday can't come quickly enough, I spend the whole week counting down the days, wondering if we'll be together in the afternoon or part ways and meet up later for the theatre. I don't think I've ever felt this excited about a person, a man.

I arrive at the ice rink a little early then feel anxious as the lesson session ends and there's no sign of Perry. But five minutes later he rushes in looking flustered.

'So sorry,' he says. 'Had a phone call about Mum just as I was leaving.' He drops the bag he is carrying down on the ground and starts to unzip it. 'Did you get your skates yet?'

'No, I thought we'd...' But I can see that he has his own and they're not the slightly smelly, scuffed ones I'm going to be wearing. 'What about your mum? Is she all right?'

'Yes, slowly improving. They're going to reduce her sedation later today. Hopefully by tomorrow when I'm there she'll be conscious.'

On the rink he's amazing, all that skating when he was a kid at his Swedish grandparents has certainly paid off.

'You skate like a pro,' I say, as he holds out his hands to guide me around the rink.

'Not really. In Sweden I'm fairly average. Here, do this, you'll find it easier.'

I follow his instructions, enjoy being in his hold, and an hour later I've only tripped over once. And even then, he caught me. I feel as though I've learnt a lot more with him than in my taster session with Angie, but that's mostly because we clung to each other for grim death.

'Shall we snatch a quick lunch?' he asks.

'Yes, great idea.'

'Then I'll need to scoot off, got a business call to make and want to check in with the hospital about Mum again.' He does a little grimace.

'I hope she's all right,' I say, fully aware of how feeble that sounds.

'Yeah, me too.'

Lunch is quick, a sandwich and a coffee in a little café around the corner, which he insists on paying for.

Outside the café we arrange a time to meet at the theatre, he also suggests that we go for dinner afterwards, which means it will be around 10pm when we eat.

'Hey,' he says, hailing a taxi. 'Are you going my way, do you want to share?'

When I tell him where I'm heading he grimaces again and shakes his head. 'Sorry, opposite direction. You take this one, I'll get another.' Before I have a chance to object he's pushing me into the taxi, gripping my hand in farewell and slamming the door. He's a true gent.

I know it's a cliché but I do love a musical. And *Back*

to the Future, the musical is just brilliant. Who doesn't love those time travel films, and throw in singing and dancing, just fantastic. My face is aching from smiling and when I glance over at Perry during the performance, his face is the same.

'Thank you so much for that,' I say, as we leave the theatre.

'Thank my client. To be honest I don't think I'd ever have thought of going to that but I did enjoy it.' He gives me a shy look. 'Must be the company.'

Now *I* feel shy.

We head off for dinner in a little restaurant he knows just off Covent Garden. They seem to know him too, and usher us to a table tucked away in the corner.

'I don't usually eat this late,' he confides in me.

'Me neither.'

'Sorry, it's just I had stuff to do. Having spent all last weekend with Mum, things have piled up.

'Do you work every day, weekends included?' I'm impressed. I'd work nonstop if the muse took me, it was partly why I was so happy for Angie to come up at weekends, it stopped me from burning out. Now I'm very disciplined.

He grins over at me. 'Not all the time. What about you?'

'I try not to work at weekends, don't always succeed.' I give a little laugh.

'You're very disingenuous Adam Hames.' He narrows his eyes at me and smiles, it's quite unnerving, as though he's found out some dirty, dark secret about me.

I find myself swallowing even though I know I've nothing to hide.

'Yes,' he says, with a little grin. 'I googled you after our first meeting and you're rather famous. RA and all that.' His eyes twinkle at me.

'Oh, yeah, that…' I shrug and try to make light of it, but I'm rather flattered that he took the time to look me up.

'Seems you hit the floor running, selling paintings while you were still at school according to *Wikipedia*.'

'Yes, well, I sold one painting to my art teacher, so you probably shouldn't believe everything you read online.' I feel a strange combination of pride and embarrassment.

'Hey,' he says, grabbing his menu. 'You should shout your achievements from on high. I do.' His eyes twinkle again.

'You're right.' I grab my menu and attempt to study it carefully.

Two hours later and we're wandering along the street in search of a taxi, we've dined and we've wined and we chatted endlessly, sharing stories about our childhoods. His sounds a lot more interesting and exciting than mine, but he tells me that mine sounds happy and loving. His parents split up when he was six and neither of them married again so he doesn't have any siblings. His father went back to Sweden and Perry sees him rarely. He tells me that I really don't know how lucky I am.

He flags down a taxi but before either of us gets in he turns to me. 'Would you like to come back for coffee?' He winks. It's so cheesy and I love it.

I nod slowly and we climb into the back of the taxi holding hands like the lovers we're about to become.

He lives in a town house, tall, pale, thin. It doesn't suit him. There's a SOLD sign outside.

'You're moving?'

'Yeah, need something more…' he shrugs and looks up and down the street. 'Suitable for me.'

'Okay.'

'Yeah, this place has been good but I need to move on now.'

'How long have you been here?" I ask, as he opens the front door.

'Too long.' He laughs.

He's right though, once we're inside I can see that the place really doesn't suit him at all. It's old fashioned but not a in cool way. He sees me take in the living room and smiles.

'Sorry, it's full of old tut. Mum downsized a few years ago and gifted me a lot of her furniture. I just haven't got round to sorting the tut from the good.' He laughs and rolls his eyes. 'Come upstairs, I do have a rather lovely chair up there, straight from Sweden.'

'Now that's a variation on come up and see my etchings. Where are you moving to?'

'Not sure. I've only just accepted an offer on this place, just yesterday actually. I've looked at a few places but not found *the one*.' He winks at me again. 'Come and see my chair.'

An offer like that is too good to miss. Of course the chair is amazing and so is he. He's definitely more experienced and a better lover than I am, I feel rather embarrassed.

'Sorry about that,' I say in the morning, when we're lying together in his not particularly comfortable bed. I've spent half the night awake worrying about my performance. This is what happens when you don't put yourself about enough.

He raises himself up on one elbow and frowns at me. 'What do you mean?'

Honestly, I love him just for that. He looks and sounds genuine. If I hadn't just experienced what I have

– my own performance in particular – I could believe he was being sincere.

'That,' I say, wishing I hadn't said anything. 'I'm somewhat out of practice.'

He grins and nudges me.

'Unlike you, who knows all the moves.'

He laughs. 'Hey, half Swedish, what can I say?' He jumps up out of bed and starts ferreting around for our clothes, picking them up off the floor and making a pile for each of us.

'I'm going for a shower,' he says, laughing. Do you care to join me?' He holds out his hand for mine.

The shower is big, as big as my own but where mine is sleek and modern this is quaint and a bit weird. There's even a grab rail on the side. He sees me looking at it.

'For my mum, when she stays in London. Another reason I need to move.'

'Was this her house then?'

'Yeah, I bought it off her when she downsized. Didn't like to say so earlier, but it's obvious, isn't it? Always intended to remodel but work just got in the way.'

'You don't fancy doing it now?'

'*Nej*,' he says. 'I want something turnkey, I'm just too busy to even think about remodelling.' He grins. 'Mustn't complain though.' His eyes twinkle as he turns on the shower taps. 'Shall we?' he asks, raising an eyebrow.

Eight

Angie has spent the entire time hounding me. From the minute she walked into my place and stomped out onto my balcony terrace she's been demanding information about Perry. What did he wear? What did he say? Where did we go? Did he pay his fair share?

I sigh before I reply which she interprets completely incorrectly.

'That bad?'

'No. We had a great time. I just don't need you to interrogate me.'

'Just looking out for you, that's all.'

'I don't need looking out for, thanks.'

She raises her eyebrows and looks to the left, it's very theatrical as well as patronising. 'You're not exactly a lothario, are you?'

'I think you'll find that lothario means a seducer of women. So no, I'm not.'

'You know what I mean. You've not had a lot of boyfriends, have you? When was the last time?'

'Enough. I'm not discussing my sex life with you.' And not just because she's hit the nail on the head.

I do wonder what I've been doing with my life with regards to relationships. Apart from fending off the

Jaspers of this world – even Gerard has had a little flirt with me – there have only been a few liaisons. Perry is like a breath of fresh air. He's exciting. He's experienced. He's already taught me things I never knew.

'Have you slept with him yet?'

'I'm not discussing that with you.'

'Which means you have.' She laughs, cuddles up to me and pats my shoulder. 'Oh, little bro, you're a man now.'

I shrug her off. 'Stop it. That's not even vaguely funny.'

'Oh, don't be like that. I'm really pleased for you, I am. And I'd like to take some credit, after all it was my idea for you to get out there. When can I meet him? This weekend?'

'No, he's away on business.'

'In Sweden? You should get him to take you with him.'

'He's already invited me.'

'Wow, that was quick. He's seducing you with Swedes.' She laughs again.

I know she's joking, and I know she means well for me, but I can't really take the teasing at the moment.

'What are we doing this weekend that doesn't involve skating?' She stands and waits for me to answer.

'It's Brent's birthday, he's having a party.'

'Fab, I love a party and fortunately for you, despite you not giving me any notice, I have brought a party frock with me. What a shame Perry can't come and meet your friends. Will Rue be there?'

'Everyone will be there, it's Brent's BIG birthday.'

'How big?'

'Four-O.' I laugh as I say it like that because that's how Brent's been saying it, or rather mouthing it as though no one knows, when everyone knows.

'Are you sure? I thought it was his fortieth last year. Didn't he rent that barge thing down the Thames especially for it?'

'No, yes, he did rent the boat, but no, he was thirty-nine.'

'I wonder what colour Rue's hair will be?'

'It was green the last time I saw her.' Acid green, it made her skin look as pale as death.

'She still best friends with *charlie*?'

'What do you think?' Poor Rue, I don't think she'll ever grow out of that, that's the consequence of too much family money and no purpose in life. She could have been a working artist; she certainly had the talent but not the ambition. 'I do worry about Rue, she won't make old bones,' I add, sounding wistful.

My sister grimaces then puts her hands together in thought. 'We should eat a proper meal before we go to the party, there'll be no food there, will there? Just booze if I remember Brent's previous parties.'

'Good idea.'

☯☯☯

We're both nursing stinking hangovers today and neither of us surfaced until after noon.

'You look like shit,' Angie says, as I slowly step across the kitchen to the coffee machine. I'm enjoying the sensation of my bare feet against the smooth, cold floor surface. It's soothing.

'Thanks. You don't look so hot yourself.'

She makes a poochy poo face at me, which is admirable because I don't think I'm capable of contorting the muscles in my face that much.

We spend the rest of the day slobbing on the sofa, eating toast and alternately drinking water and coffee until by 5pm we're both almost human. We've hardly spoken but we have watched – if that is the right word – several episodes of Breaking Bad on *Netflix*, which we've both already seen which makes it easier to follow with a hangover.

Angie disappears off for a shower and while she's gone my phone rings.

'Hey, how's it going?' Perry's voice brings a smile to my face. I'm glad Angie is not here right this minute or she'd be snatching the phone off me.

'Cool. What about you?' I'm certainly not telling him I have the mother of all hangovers.

'Oh, stuck in an airport at the moment, but I should touch down in London later this evening. Would you like to meet me at my place?' He giggles, it makes me laugh.

I think about his request, it would be an easy thing to do. I'll have to shower and dress to drop Angie off anyway. However, the thought of sleeping in that lumpy bed is definitely not appealing.

'Hey,' I say, mimicking him. 'Why don't you stay here tonight, with me.'

'Oh, okay. You'll need to give me the address.'

'Better still, I'll pick you up. Text me your flight details and I'll be waiting.'

'Okay.' I hear the smile in his voice. 'So what have you been up to this weekend while I've been working?'

'Went to a party, a fortieth birthday party.'

'Whose?'

'Brent, my close friend.'

'Oh?' There's a tone to his voice and I know what he's thinking.

'Don't worry, he's straight. He's looking forward to

meeting you though, everyone is.'

I hadn't planned on telling anyone about Perry. It's early days and you never know how these things will pan out. When the time is right I do plan to introduce him to all my friends, but that time isn't now. I was keeping him as my own lovely little secret but not any longer. Big mouth Angie couldn't keep it shut, especially after she'd had a few wines and, although she denied it, a quick visit to the loo with Rue. They both had that saucer-eyed look that can mean only one thing, especially where Rue is concerned, *charlie* sniffing. I don't do drugs, drink is bad enough, but cocaine is a definite no no.

Angie has told them all that once we all have a weekend free she'll organise a nice dinner party for everyone to meet Perry. She means she'll organise a party at my place and have catering staff in, paid for, of course, by me, unless our guests are happy eating beans on toast or lasagne which are the only part of Angie's culinary repertoire worth mentioning, which I doubt. At first I was annoyed, but I've warmed to the idea. It's far too soon yet, but at some point I want him to meet my friends and I want to meet his.

'Yeah, we had a fun weekend.'

'Cool,' Perry says. 'But it'll just be you and me this evening, won't it?'

'Absolutely.'

'Great, because I'm exhausted and I just want to spend my time chilling with you, not sharing you.'

'It'll just be us.'

☯☯☯

My skin tingles as I watch Perry saunter out of the airport. There's something about the way he walks, confident but not arrogant. He scans the numerous parked cars looking for mine, that's when I realise he doesn't actually know what I drive because he's never seen it. Just as I'm about to jump out and wave to him he spots me and marches over.

'Hey,' he says, as he climbs into the passenger seat before leaning over and kissing me on the lips.

I like it, but I feel slightly embarrassed; public displays of affection have never been my thing and even though you could argue that inside my car isn't public, it feels it. His breath tastes salty.

'Peanuts and lager on the plane,' he says, making me suddenly aware that I'm licking my lips. 'Sorry.' He grins.

'Not much of a meal.'

'No, didn't fancy anything else.'

'It's not too late to get something. What would you fancy?'

He grins again. It's very disarming. 'You,' he says.

I start the engine and focus on pulling out of the line of waiting cars. I swallow hard. He grabs and squeezes my knee gently, it's friendly.

'Hey, I could do with a shower when we get to yours.'

'Of course.'

'Maybe you could join me.'

I keep my eyes on the road. I know we've already shared a shower at his but the remnants of my hangover are still lingering.

'I've just had a shower.'

He laughs, squeezes my knee again then lets go and leans back in his seat. 'I'm shattered,' he says.

I park in the underground garage and we take the lift straight up to my place. We don't need to go via the reception which is just as well as I'd feel slightly embarrassed, although I doubt it's a secret or even a surprise to anyone that I'm gay. I don't know why I feel like this with Perry, Jasper who is so very camp, pops up to see me all the time.

Once we step through the door Perry's mouth drops open.

'Hey, no wonder you wanted me to come here. This place…' He stops speaking, lets go of his luggage, spreads his arms and spins around. The action reminds me a little of Angie. 'It's fantastic, ja?'

'Ja,' I repeat.

He laughs. 'What must you think of me in my house full of granny furniture?' He laughs again.

I shrug. My parents always told us that if you can't say anything nice then say nothing; we were brought up properly. While I don't always practise this maxim, I am with Perry.

'This is what I want, do many come up for sale?'

I shake my head. I cannot remember the last time one was sold.

'This is the penthouse, ja?'

'Ja.'

He laughs again. 'Sorry, I've spent too much time in Sweden lately and it comes out when I'm tired. Do they go on the open market when they sell, or is it very hush hush?'

'I don't know. Only ever seen one sold since I moved in.'

'Is this the only penthouse?'

'No, there are two.'

'Hey, imagine if I lived next door.'

I am imagining if he lived here with me. He looks good in my apartment, it suits him.

'Is that the river?' he asks, striding towards the doors. Below us the lights on the little boats sailing the Thames twinkle. 'So cool. I want what you've got.' I think he means my apartment, but then he winks. 'Hey, show me this shower.'

He never makes it into the shower because he spots the bath first. It's double ended and freestanding. I have to admit that I rarely use it, but when he suggests we share it, I find myself unable to refuse. Before I know what's happening he is washing my hair, and soon I am washing his. It's long, and surprises me because despite looking silky it's quite coarse.

'Put plenty of conditioner on,' he says. 'All this flying in plane atmospheres dries it out.'

I do as I'm told and lather it on then massage it in. He leans into me, his back to my chest.

'That feels so good.'

It does. I feel like the lead in a romantic film. I also feel faintly ridiculous but not enough to stop.

☯☯☯

He wakes me up the next morning, it's barely 8am. He's fully dressed, even has his coat on.

'Oh, right.' I sit up, my intention to get up and at least make him breakfast.

'Hey, Adam, stay in bed. Rest.' He smiles at me fondly. 'I have to go, business meeting in the City then I need to go and see my mum.'

I suddenly realise I haven't asked after her, haven't even thought about her. 'How is she?'

'Getting there. Hospital have done everything they can. Going to discuss rehab today.' He comes towards me, sits on the bed. 'Hey, you did an excellent job on my hair last night, so I didn't get it wet in the shower this morning.' He shakes his head and swishes his hair across his shoulders. 'See, feel it.'

He grabs my hand and strokes his hair with it. It's both funny and erotic. He jumps up from the bed.

'I'll ring you when I know what I'm doing, maybe get together later in the week?'

'Yes. Do you want a lift somewhere?' I pull the duvet away.

'No, no, I've booked an Uber. Goodbye, *min kärlek*.' The last two words run into each other and I don't know what they mean, something nice I hope. Then he's gone.

I grab my phone and spend a ludicrous amount of time googling what he said, spelling it all ways until finally I find what I think it is. It definitely doesn't sound like it looks.

It means my love.

And I think I might just be a little bit in love too, with Perry Oblekt.

Nine

To be fair I didn't expect to hear from Perry on Monday. But by Tuesday evening I was getting a little… what? Annoyed? Concerned? By Wednesday morning I rang and left him a voicemail. Nothing heavy, just a quick message asking how he was, how his mum was. He didn't reply.

Angie, on the other hand, has messaged me daily, though mercifully not about Perry. She's coming up at the weekend, it'll be nice to see her. I was going to tell her how Perry stayed over, how fantastic it's been between us, now I'm not so sure.

It's Friday morning, it's early, well before seven, but I'm awake. I've been working on a commissioned piece all week and I hope to finish it today. I've skipped breakfast and I'm just starting in the studio when my phone flashes with an incoming call. I snatch it up from the table.

'Hey, Adam, sorry I missed your call.' Perry's voice sounds strained.

'No problem,' I say. 'How's things?' I'm trying to sound casual.

'Oh, you know. I've had to sort things out for Mum but hopefully okay now. Have you plans for the weekend?'

I hesitate a moment too long.

'Don't worry if you do, some other time.' He sounds deflated.

'Um, my plans aren't set in stone.' Though *I* might be if I cancel Angie again.

'It's just I have to go to Sweden again tonight and I wondered if you wanted to come. Flying visit but need to do a bit of business.'

Of course I want to go to Sweden. It's one place I've never been, all my holidays and there have been many, have been in typical hot countries; Barbados, Seychelles, Mauritius. 'What's the weather like there?' I ask.

'At this time of year a little bit colder than here.' He laughs. 'It's not the North Pole, not yet anyway.'

'I'd love to come.' I just have to put Angie off.

We make arrangements and I abandon my painting for a while to sort out my packing, he tells me to bring a carry-on case so we don't have to queue for baggage. I message over a photo of my passport so he can book my ticket. If I can get everything ready now, I can finish my work without clock watching constantly, although I do have to be at the airport by five.

By mid-afternoon the painting is finished and I ring Jasper to tell him. I also tell him I'm going away for the weekend. He's intrigued and questions me but I'm vague in my response. I don't want Jasper gossiping about me and Perry to all and sundry, although of course, thanks to Angie, he knows Perry exists.

'I'll send someone over to pick up the painting tomorrow. Good job I have a key.' I can almost hear him rolling his eyes. 'We need to ship it all the way to Scotland, they want it early next week.' He laughs as though Scotland is on the other side of the world.

'Whereabouts again?'

'Glasgow. You have remembered to sign it, haven't you? We know what you're like.'

'I have,' I say, wandering over to the painting and checking. 'Bottom right-hand corner.'

'Excellent. Send me a photo, so I can make sure they pick up the right one.'

'You will be with them, I hope.'

'Of course, dear boy, of course. Have a great weekend.' He ends the call and I wonder if he's being honest with me.

I hope he's not going to give the key to some courier company. I'd have a word with the concierge, Martin, but he rarely works weekends, it'll be one of those agency guys.

I have an hour before I need to leave so, despite putting it off as long as possible, I have to call Angie.

She doesn't answer and her phone goes to voicemail; I leave a message for her to ring me urgently.

I'm in the taxi on the way to the airport when she rings back.

'What's so urgent?' she asks, sounding irritated, her voice barely above a whisper.

'Why are you whispering?'

'Because they don't like us making personal calls during work hours so I'm hiding in the loos. What's the problem?'

'Something's come up last minute, I won't be around this weekend.' There, I've said it.

'What's come up?'

'A trip to Sweden.' I clench my teeth together waiting but there's a long silence on the other end of the phone. Then I hear a toilet flush.

'Sorry, someone came in but they've gone now.'

'That was quick.'

'Cleaner, I think, checking the soap and paper towels, flushing the loos where others can't be bothered.'

'Urgh.'

'Never mind that, tell me about Sweden. I assume you're going with Perry.'

'I am.'

'Going to meet his family? And he hasn't even met any of yours, especially me, and we're in this country, basically on your doorstep, sometimes in your flat.'

'I don't know if I'm meeting his family.' At least he hasn't said anything to suggest I will be. 'He's there on business.'

'Right. Well have a fab time. What about me?'

'You can't really come with us.'

'I know that. But I was coming up tomorrow.'

'You could still come. That could work out quite well as Jasper is supposed to be collecting a painting but I think he might just send a courier.'

'Oh, I see, you just want me there for admin purposes.'

'No, not at all. What I mean is...'

She cuts across my words with a loud cackle. 'I know,' she says, reverting back to a whisper. 'Yeah, okay. You won't have to reimburse me for my train ticket either if I use it because I've already bought it.' She's a cheeky bitch.

'Win win, then,' I say. 'Got to go, just arriving at the airport. Speak soon. Don't forget your key, you always forget your key. See you next weekend.'

'Yeah, yeah. Take photos,' she says, as I end the call.

Perry is waiting for me as I climb out of the taxi. He waves and smiles as he hurries towards me. We hug awkwardly, my fault.

'Let's go,' he says. 'Got your passport? We can do boarding passes on the machine then head straight through to the departure lounge.'

We scuttle along, dragging our wheelies behind us. When he wants to Perry can certainly move fast.

'Are we in a rush?' I ask, when we reach security.

'Not really.' He smiles. 'Sorry, did you struggle to keep up?'

'No. Just wondered if we were late.'

'Not at all, *min kärlek*. They want our passports.' He gestures at me. 'After you.'

I'm relieved that we're flying business class. I always fly business class or better because I can afford it, but I haven't paid for my seat, Perry has.

'How much do I owe you?' I whisper into his ear once we are seated.

'For what?'

'My flight.'

'Oh, nothing. My treat.' He grips my hand and smiles as the plane starts to taxi towards the runway. His face has gone quite white. 'No matter how often I fly I still hate take off.' He squeezes my hand and I squeeze back.

He performs several breathing exercises as the plane rises into the sky and I begin to wonder if he thinks he's giving birth. I can't help smiling.

'What's funny?' he gasps, between breaths.

'Nothing, really nothing.'

'You think I'm melodramatic.'

'Maybe.' Now I feel mean.

'I was involved in a plane crash once.'

Now I feel cruel for laughing. 'I'm so sorry, obviously not fatal.' I sound flippant, however unintentional.

'Not for me,' he says, grimacing.

Finally the plane levels out and Perry lets go of my

hand. Without thinking I give it a quick shake to get the blood flowing again.

'Sorry,' he says.

'Not a problem. I understand. What happened?'

'I can't talk about it. PTSD,' he mutters, turning away.

I suppose it would do that to anyone, being in a plane crash, surviving when others didn't.

'Let's have champagne,' he says, when the steward comes round. 'Let's celebrate us and getting into the air safely and pray for a safe landing.'

The steward raises an eyebrow before opening the champagne and pouring us a glass each.

'Let's not eat on the plane, I want to take you to one of my favourite restaurants.'

By the time we land in Stockholm we're both starving and the first thing we do once out of the airport is grab a taxi and find the restaurant. The one he has chosen offers a panoramic view of both Lake Mälaren and inner-city Stockholm. We sit outside. It's quite enchanting even if we do have to stuff our wheelie cases under the table to prevent people tripping over them.

Perry hands over a menu and waits while I try to decipher it. He smiles as he watches me frown.

'What's this?' I ask, pointing to the first item.

'Well, it's a sort of fish wrapped…' He smiles. 'Hey, let me chose for you.'

'Umm…' I'm a little reluctant.

'Yes, I know what you like. I'll pick well for you.' He grins, calls the waitress over and after a short conversation with her hands our menus back.

Minutes later two bottles of beer arrive.

'To my darling Adam, *min kärlek,*' he says, clinking his bottle with mine.

'To us.' This seems so very romantic, sitting in the

cool night air sipping beer in Stockholm. 'That's good.'

'*Omnipollo Nebuchadnezzar*,' he says, rolling the words around his tongue before laughing. 'Sweden's most famous beer. Started off as home brew and was so popular…' He grins. 'Oh, and strong.'

'Yes, I can feel it hitting the spot. I'll be glad when we eat.' The beer, on top of the champagne is quite the heady mix.

When the food arrives I am relieved to see that he has chosen well for me, no odd pickled herring or whatever I imagine the Swedes eat. Just good old red meat in a rich sauce. We chat about the food, about Stockholm, about how thrilled we both are that I was available to come here at such short notice. I only feel a little tinge of guilt about putting Angie off, but, as I reassured her, there will be plenty of other weekends.

After we've eaten we jump into another taxi.

I'm a little disappointed when we pull up outside a hotel, albeit a very luxurious one. Perry sees my face.

'What's wrong.'

'Nothing. Really nothing.'

'If the hotel is not to your liking, we can find another.'

'No, no, it looks very high end.'

He smiles then. 'It is. I always stay here when I'm in town.'

'I suppose a little part of me hoped we might be staying with your family.' There, it's said, that's the trouble with too much alcohol, it loosens the tongue.

'Ah, I see. No, no. My family don't live in the city, they live miles out and along the coast. There won't be time for us to travel there this weekend but another time we must visit and stay with them. They have plenty of room. To be honest it's a place best visited in high summer when the nights are short and the days are very,

very long.'

He chuckles to himself as he chats to the receptionist as she books us in and summons an aide to take us to our room which turns out to be a suite and is rather sumptuous. Would it be rubbing salt in the wound if I sent a photo to Angie?

Before long we're snuggled up in the immense bed and Perry is whispering sweet nothings in my ear.

☯☯☯

In the morning he dresses in a suit and tie.

'So formal,' I say, as he wheels over the breakfast cart which has just been delivered.

'I know. I'm sorry. I have a business meeting this morning. It's only a small company but the owner is old and very formal. He expects respect and this is how he perceives it.'

'I see. How long will you be?'

'I should be back by lunch time. If you want to go out without me just ask at the reception for a map and some directions. Or you can wait for me, spend some time in that jacuzzi pool in the bathroom. I can put the do not disturb sign on the door when I leave.'

'Okay.'

'And then I have a surprise for you. I hope.' He starts to eat his breakfast hurriedly.

'What is it?'

'Ah, it wouldn't be a surprise now, would it? Ja?'

After he's gone I find the TV remote and flick through the channels but since I don't speak Swedish it's rather pointless so I take that jacuzzi bath and by noon I am bored stupid by this lovely room. By one there's still no sign of Perry so I message him. He doesn't reply. By two I'm starting to worry that something has happened to him and send another message, this time rather frantic sounding.

At two-thirty he bursts in through the door, pink faced and panting.

'Are you all right?'

'Yes, sorry. It just took longer than I expected, but worth it. I'll just change then we'll get off for the surprise.'

Ten

'Surprise?' I ask, a little hesitant.

'You're going to love it,' Perry says, as he starts to peel off his work clothes before disappearing into the bathroom.

He's soon back and pulling on clean clothes. He looks good in dark jeans and a white t-shirt. He grins at me as he pulls on a jacket, finds his wallet and holds out his hand for me.

'Ready?'

'Have been for hours.' I didn't mean that to sound as miserable as it does.

'I'm sorry,' he says. 'I truly am. It was sort of worth it but not to upset you.'

I nod quietly. How can I sulk when he's here now, with me?

Once out of the hotel I stop as I expect him to ask the doorman to hail a taxi, but Perry turns about and frowns at me. 'This way,' he says. 'It isn't far.'

He's right, no sooner have we started walking that we stop.

'Abba, the museum.' I am definitely surprised.

'Don't you just love it?' He grabs my arm and starts marching us towards the entrance. When I don't answer he stops and turns to me. 'You do like Abba, don't you?'

'Umm, yeah, sure.' How can I say anything else?

'Thank God, because these tickets cost me a fortune.' He laughs. 'Anyway, I've never met a gay man who doesn't love Abba.'

He marches us in and off we go; it's an interactive experience and we virtually try on costumes, sing songs and almost become our favourite Abba members, not that I really have one. Perry is Benny and I am Bjorn. I do enjoy it, mainly because I'm with Perry who is absolutely loving it and is fully immersed in the whole experience. However, despite being gay, I'm not a big Abba fan. I don't hate them; I just don't love them. But it's been a fun afternoon especially as I've fed off Perry's enthusiasm.

Eventually we reach the inevitable giftshop. He insists on buying us both a t-shirt. His says 'The Winner Takes It All', mine says 'Dancing Queen'. I really don't know when I will wear that.

We drift over to the vinyl section where Perry starts looking through the records.

'Have you got a deck?' he asks.

'Deck? No, no I don't,' I say, realising what he means. The last thing I want is him buying me an Abba album.

'Me neither. Shame.' He grins and nudges me along. 'I'm starving, haven't eaten since breakfast. What about you?'

'Same.'

'Great, let's snatch an early dinner.'

He marches us back around to the hotel and we go straight in for dinner.

☯☯☯

We ate and drank rather too much last night but it was fun. Perry is great company. He has a funny story to tell about almost everything. When he started crooning Abba songs in the bar I knew it was time for us to go to our room.

He's in the shower now, he's still singing Abba songs, currently an underwater version of *The Winner Takes It All* is seeping out from under the bathroom door.

When he comes out, wrapped in a hotel robe and dabbing his lovely, blond hair dry, he smiles at me.

'Since you didn't enjoy the Abba treat, I have something planned which I'm sure you're going to like.'

'I didn't say I didn't enjoy it…' I start.

He laughs. 'You need to tell your face that.' He yanks the bedcovers off me. 'Go, shower. We need to get off soon, we've slept in a bit later than I expected. We'll have to skip breakfast.'

I'm soon ready because unlike Perry who has to spend a lot of time adding product to and drying his hair, I'm fairly low maintenance. I keep my hair short because it's easy.

We're standing outside the hotel watching as our taxi approaches. I've searched my brain for another Swedish pop band but can't think of any, so hopefully this isn't another Abba type surprise. Even as I'm thinking this I feel ungrateful but remind myself that I haven't said as much to Perry, although, apparently he knows. Whatever today brings I am going to smile until my jaw aches. Just being with Perry is enough for me, it truly is.

We pull up outside the Vasa Museum. I find myself wondering if Vasa are a pop group. Surely not, I would have heard of them, wouldn't I?

'What do you think?' Perry asks, his face earnest.

'Looks impressive.'

'You've never heard of it?'

'No,' I confess.

'You're going to love it.'

After he pays for the taxi we head for the entrance.

'Let me pay for this,' I say, aware that he spent a fortune yesterday.

'Certainly not. This is my treat.' He pulls out his wallet as we approach the ticket booth.

'Oh, wow,' I say, having glanced around the entrance hall while he's paying, I now know what this place is about.

'Come on.' He grabs my arm and pulls me in. 'This way,' he says. 'You've got to see this.'

I'm silent, my mouth open as I stare at the ship.

'It's seventeenth century,' Perry tells me. 'Was in the sea for over three-hundred years before they salvaged it in the sixties. She has sixty-four guns and sunk on her maiden voyage.' He grins at me. 'Do you love it?'

'I do.' I really do. It's fascinating.

Hours pass as we wander around the ship marvelling at the workmanship and the restoration. There are hundreds of carved figures across the back and sides of the ship, the detail is incredible. On the ground floor is a scale model of the ship showing how it would have looked when new, the colours are brilliant. My artist's eye goes straight to the detail, the minutiae of each figure. I could spend days here and never be bored. We're just about to move onto the figurehead when Perry pulls at my arm.

'There's a restaurant here,' he says. 'Aren't you hungry? I know I am.' He grimaces before laughing.

'Oh, yes, sure. I am. It's just…' I look around me, awestruck.

'I knew you'd love it. Come on, let's eat before I faint

away. Then we can come back and continue.' He scuttles towards the restaurant signs and pulls me along behind him. I suspect that Perry feels the same about the Vasa Museum as I felt about the Abba Museum yesterday.

The things we do for love, I think. If that's what's this is.

I love him just for bringing me here, this is a treat I would never have experienced.

Despite being starving and having no breakfast we opt for a light lunch because Perry has booked us 'somewhere lovely' for dinner. I try to pay for lunch but he insists I cannot. I've never met anyone so generous, even Jasper who earns from me is sometimes reluctant to foot the bill and will never argue if I offer despite our lunches always being his idea and allegedly to discuss business.

We head back into the museum and by the time the place closes and we are the last to leave, we both have aching legs.

Once we're back in our hotel room Perry flops onto the bed and I follow suit, kicking off my shoes in the process.

'That was the best day ever,' I say, leaning over and kissing him on the cheek. 'Thank you.'

'Hey, I know. Eh? Don't let me fall asleep because we have to be at the restaurant by seven.'

Despite the restaurant definitely being lovely and the food amazing we're both yawning our heads off by nine pm.

'We may as well head back,' Perry says. '*Jag är trött,*' he says, leaning back and stretching his arms.

'What does that mean?' Is it another term of endearment?

'Sorry, when I hear everyone around us speaking

Swedish I just fall in with them. It means I'm tired. We have an early flight tomorrow, need to be at the airport before eight. But at least we can eat on the plane. I really don't like to have breakfast too early.'

'Shame we have to leave so early but thank you for the most amazing weekend.'

'Abba notwithstanding,' he says, grinning at me.

'I enjoyed it because you did.'

'Ah, I see. And I enjoyed the Vasa because you did, just as I knew you would.' He reaches over and grips my hand, then lets go and calls the waiter over for the bill.

We have another wrestle over who is paying but in the end I give up and let him pay.

Before we go to bed Perry rings down and organises a taxi for the morning.

☯☯☯

Our brilliant weekend is over. I'm sorry to be saying goodbye to Stockholm.

'Hey,' Perry says. 'Don't look so glum. There will be other weekends.'

'Of course.' I smile brightly. 'Are you about this week?'

'Not really. I'm still sorting my mum out. The NHS rehab isn't going to cut the mustard.' He grimaces. 'I need to find somewhere better.'

'I'm sorry. I thought it was all sorted, you never said.'

'No problem. I don't like to dwell on it. But only the best for Mum. I just want to get her back to normal. At least as near normal as possible. She wants to go home, bless her. I also have to work, as I'm sure you do.' He smiles at me.

'I do.' I've had several texts from Jasper telling me the

painting that was collected on Saturday was delivered on Sunday and the client was so thrilled that he wants two others in a similar vein. I need to get cracking because he wants them by the end of the month. He's throwing some great party then. It really shouldn't be a problem. And, as Jasper has pointed out, he's prepared to pay a premium for the short turnaround.

On the plane we eat breakfast in subdued silence, neither of us particularly keen to get back to real life.

We take a taxi together from the airport, and I am dropped off first. Perry insists on paying again; this weekend has cost me nothing other than my taxi to the airport. It seems very wrong. It's not as though I can't afford to pay my way. And some.

Once home I feel at a loss. I immediately message Perry and thank him for a fantastic time.

He doesn't reply even though I can see that he's received and read it.

Angie, however, messages me frequently throughout the day. I send her photos of the Abba and the Vasa experiences.

Angie: *20 photos of popstars and a crusty old ship and none of either of you. Where's the couple selfie? Or even a one of Perry? Send now.*

Me: *I didn't take any. Never crossed my mind.*

It's true, it didn't, which seems ridiculous on reflection. We were just so busy enjoying ourselves.

Angie: *Never mind, I'll get to meet him in person at the weekend.*

Me: *You will.*

I hope she will. Perry and I haven't agreed anything for the weekend, I've assumed he'll be available because he's busy all week and a man has to have some time off. Even Perry.

It's ten at night when Perry finally replies to say he had a great time too. I message back and tell him that my sister is desperate to meet him and we both hope it will be this weekend.

He rings me.

'Hey, *min kärlek,*' he starts. 'About the weekend, I wasn't going to say anything yet but have to now. I want to take you away.'

'Again?' I say, aware that the word might have come out not quite as I intended.

'Hey, you don't want to go away with me?'

'Yes, of course I do.'

'Amsterdam,' he says. 'It will be two weekends and the whole week in between. I have business but I want to spend as much time with you. Will you be able to come? Say you will, *min kärlek.*'

'This weekend?'

'Yes, but leave Saturday rather than Friday. Back the following Sunday.'

'Um, yes, okay.' Mentally I'm working out how much work I can get done before I go away. I've got almost three weeks but I will be losing over a week in the middle.

'I'll send the details over,' he says. 'And I'll pick you up in a taxi on Saturday. I might not be around much between now and then, but message me if you feel the need.' He almost giggles.

'Enough of that,' I say. 'I'm sure I won't feel the need.'

'Well, you never know. Speak soon. Goodbye, Adam.'

And he's gone.

Eleven

Angie was very disappointed but also very understanding, that was after she gave me the lecture about not rushing into things too quickly. I had to remind her again that I'm an adult. I've also told her it's time she found herself a boyfriend because then she wouldn't be so interested in mine.

I'm definitely ready for a break by the time Perry picks me up in a taxi on Saturday morning. I've worked solidly all week doing as much as I can to move the two commissioned pieces on. It's amazing how having a tough deadline spurs both creativity and productivity. Jasper came over yesterday to check on my progress. He was impressed.

'Will these match the original,' he asked.

'What do you think?'

'Well, I mean, you don't have the original.'

'I took plenty of photos.' I pointed over to the laptop open on my studio desk, it was displaying the original.

He wandered over and inspected it carefully, glancing back and forth comparing the two. 'Only he's having a big party and these three will be displayed on the same wall, as a trio.'

'Don't you think they match then?'

'Yeah, looks like it on the computer.'

'But you saw the original…'

He performed a tiny little shrug followed by a head nod, also tiny.

'You didn't, did you? You sent someone else to collect it. The courier. You gave my key to the courier.'

'Don't worry, dear boy, I have it back. How else could I have let myself in today?'

'I don't want you giving out my key to all and sundry. Why did you do that?'

'They signed in with the guard, Martin, is it?'

'He's not a guard and Martin doesn't work weekends.'

'They still signed in and out with…' he flaps his arms. 'Whoever.'

'I'm not happy about it, any of it. Fortunately Angie was here so she oversaw your couriers, but you weren't to know that.'

'I'm not happy about you disappearing off for over a week in the middle of a big commission, but there we are.' His tone screamed annoyance.

'I'm going on holiday, a well-earned break.'

'With your new boyfriend.' He smiled then; it wasn't a particularly nice smile. 'In the middle of a big commission, a very well-paid commission,' he added.

I'm still smarting about that conversation with Jasper when I get into the taxi. Perry leans over and hugs me.

'Excited?'

'Yeah,' I say.

'Better tell your face then.'

'Sorry,' I say, before telling him about my encounter with Jasper yesterday.

'You let him have a key to your apartment and he just waltzes in whenever he pleases?'

It does sound faintly ridiculous now he says it.

'Who else has a key?'

'Just my sister but she's family so doesn't count.'

This causes him to raise an eyebrow. 'Let's hope the couriers haven't made copies and sold them on the dark web.'

'What? No.' Now he's overreacting.

'Not too likely, I'll admit, but possible. He should have left your key with the concierge and have them use it then return it on their way out.' He pauses. 'Ah, but the concierge could have sold a copy on the dark web.' He grins at me.

'Stop it. You're making me paranoid. Angie was there, although she left them to it. If I'd told Jasper Angie was there he wouldn't have needed to give the couriers the key. My own fault really.'

'Too many keys floating about. You need to be more careful. Do you have an alarm?'

'No, no, because we have a building concierge.'

'Maybe we need to rethink your security,' he says, reaching for my hand. 'I wouldn't want anything happening to *min kärlek*.'

☯☯☯

The hotel Perry has chosen is exquisite; boutique and luxurious and no doubt expensive. Of course we have a suite which includes a giant bathtub and a separate sitting room, there's even a private terrace overlooking the garden. We argue about me making a contribution but he absolutely insists that I do not.

Once we've unpacked our cases and claimed our territory, he pulls out a printed list of dates.

'Is this our itinerary?' I ask, taking the sheet of paper from him.

'Sort of. Well, no. It's the times and dates I have meetings booked for.'

'Ah.' I scan the page, there seem to be quite a lot. I feel deflated.

'I'm sorry, *min kärlek*, but mine is a business that cannot be left to its own devices, especially now when I am growing it.'

'Of course. Is there much Swedish furniture here then?' Apart from *IKEA*, I think.

He tilts his head from side to side. 'Demand is such that I'm having to diversify,' he says, grinning.

'Okay. Sounds good.' I think.

He pulls out a guidebook from his bag and brings it over to me. I'm sitting on the sofa now clutching the paper. He sits next to me, puts his arm around my shoulder.

'I've been to Amsterdam many times, but there are still places I haven't been. Since you've never been I thought you would like to fill all the gaps in my schedule. Book somewhere for us to visit every day. But give me an hour or so after meetings to travel. That way I won't be late.'

'Okay.' I take the guidebook and half-heartedly flick through it.

Perry watches me carefully before pulling out his wallet. 'Most can be booked online,' he says, taking out a credit card and pressing it into my hand. 'Use this one,' he says.

'I can pay,' I say, pushing the card away.

'No. Absolutely not. You must use mine. I have dragged you away from your work to be with me, the least you can do is let me pay.' He smiles.

'Okay.' I make a mental note to treat him at some point in the future.

Right then his phone rings, the shrill ring tone breaking the slightly tense atmosphere in the room. He glances at the screen.

'Excuse me, I must take this.'

He answers then wanders off into the bedroom silently closing the door behind him.

He's probably no more than five minutes but during that time I flick through the guidebook, pull out my phone and use it to make a list.

'Sorry, that was about Mum.'

'Is she okay?' I ask, suddenly aware that I haven't asked until now, which is remiss of me yet again. What must he think?

'Yes, she's settled well into the rehab place and now that they've been able to do a proper assessment over a few days, they've just told me she'll be there a while.'

'But she'll be okay?'

'Well, mostly, eventually. They think she'll need to be there at least a month. She'd better be good when she comes out because that place is costing me a fortune. Not that I begrudge it, she's worth every penny.'

'Then you must let me pay for our excursions here.' I reach for his credit card to give it back to him.

'No. Absolutely not, no. I'll be offended if you attempt to pay for anything.'

I can tell by the look on his face that it's no good arguing with him. He glances at the guidebook which I've placed face down to keep my place.

'Hey, so, what have you planned for this afternoon?'

'Um, well, I hadn't yet.'

He grins. 'Come on, pick somewhere.'

We spend the afternoon at the Anne Frank House, it's very sobering when we take the tour. Afterwards, outside, we exchange a look and both take a deep breath.

'Enough culture,' Perry says, grabbing my hand. 'What we need now is food and drink.'

And so the pattern of our time in Amsterdam is set. I book us tickets for tourist attractions for while we're together and when I'm on my own I visit art galleries. There are so many to choose from, the Rijksmuseum, the Van Gogh, the Moco, the Rembrandthuis, the list is endless and every day I visit somewhere different. As an artist myself I cannot believe that I have never been here before. There was, if I remember rightly, a trip here when I was at art school, but I had broken my leg skiing the previous week, so couldn't go. And now I'm marvelling at what I missed. Why did I never make the time to come after that, why did no one really impress upon me how important a visit would be? This place is a like a gift from the gods for any artist.

Selfishly, I haven't included any art galleries in the list of visits for Perry and I together. He says he doesn't mind, which is kind of him as I much prefer absorbing the art on my own, without listening to comments from the uninformed, which Perry happily admits he is.

The week flies by; Angie pesters me for photos and I reply with shots of tourist attractions and the odd painting, the ones I'm allowed to photograph.

Angie: *I want selfies of you and Perry, not crusty old masters. I'm beginning to think your boyfriend is imaginary.*

It transpires that Perry hates having his photo taken, really hates, not just dislikes it. He's almost phobic about it. I capture a sly one of us at dinner one evening with the intention of sending it to Angie later. But when I come to send it later there's no sign of it, which is odd, I suppose it didn't come out. When I tell Angie this via text, she suggests that maybe he's a vampire. She's such a comedian, my sister.

We arrive home early on Sunday evening and I invite Perry to stay over. Having spent over a week with him I'm reluctant to let him go. He tells me he feels the same.

On Monday morning he has to leave early, go back to his place and jet back off to Sweden again, although not Stockholm this time. He asks me if I would like to come. I'd love to, but I can't because I have work to do. I'm going to have to work flat out from now until the paintings are collected. Sadly, this also means the weekend and that means that Angie cannot come up, and ideally – though not ideal – I won't be seeing Perry.

He tells me he understands. While he confesses that he does not have an artistic bone in his body – I'm not sure about that – he understands that work is work, especially for the self-employed, which we both are. He rings me most evenings and I even remember to ask about his mum, who is, apparently, progressing as well as can be expected. I suggest he could come over in the evenings when he's back in the UK and he says he'd love to, but won't be able to until after I've finished my commission anyway. Which works out rather well.

Angie is disappointed she can't come up and so am I. It feels as though I haven't seen her for ages. And although we chat on the phone and I tell her about Amsterdam, it isn't the same.

Jasper comes over a few days before the paintings are due to be collected. He inspects my work, peering closely at the brush strokes and declaring they are probably better than the original one.

'You can be a cheeky sod sometimes,' I tell him.

He doesn't respond to my comment, doesn't even acknowledge it. 'Maybe your time in Amsterdam wasn't such a waste.'

'It wasn't a waste at all on any level.'

'But the art there… I had no idea you'd never been. I just assumed… Well, every great artist does the Dutch art museums in their youth, why didn't you?'

I sigh. I can't even be bothered to reply.

'What did your boyfriend think of the art?' His words are said in a nasty tone and again I don't dignify them with a response.

When he leaves in a slight huff, I'm relieved. The paintings are being collected mid-morning on Monday and I've told him in no uncertain terms that since I will be here he does not need to lend my key to anyone.

By lunchtime on Monday, the paintings having been packed and sent on their way so I'm feeling at a loose end when Perry rings.

'Hey,' he starts. 'Are you free this afternoon?'

'I could be.'

'Great. I have to go house hunting now, as a matter of urgency. My buyers want to accelerate the move. I've been a bit lazy in looking and busy with work of course, but now I must find somewhere quickly.'

'I'd love to come and look with you.'

'Great, I've lined up two to see today. There's nothing in your block advertised, but could you ask your concierge? They usually know what's going on.'

'I will.'

'Cool, can you drive? Pick me up in an hour?'

'I can.'

Twelve

The first property we view is in a fantastic location but needs a complete refurbishment.

'I love it,' Perry says. 'But I couldn't live in this while it was being refurbed.'

'No,' I agree. I do like the way it looks out over the river but from a different perspective to mine. 'I think with binoculars we could see my place,' I quip.

Standing on a balcony very much smaller than mine, Perry squints into the distance. 'I think you may be right.' He turns to the estate agent. 'Okay, we'll meet you at the next one.' He sighs before addressing his next remark to me. 'I really fancied this on paper but I couldn't live with that kitchen, could you?'

I glance over at the shabby door leading into a tiny kitchenette affair. 'No. It all needs knocking through. It could be amazing.'

The agent glances between us. 'It's a very good price for the area, reflecting the level of work that needs doing.'

Perry nods. I smile.

The agent continues to talk. 'Is this your first home together?'

We laugh. Perry says, 'No.'

I don't answer.

We both sigh as soon as we enter the next property. It's been fully refurbished and while it's certainly not to my taste it's a damn sight better than where Perry currently lives.

'What do you think?' I ask him.

He rolls his eyes. 'Not for me,' he says as he wanders into the kitchen. 'Better suited to a family, I think,' he says to the agent, who seems to suppress the urge to roll her eyes judging by the way her face contorts.

We both leave feeling a little despondent.

Back at my place Perry lounges on the sofa and pulls out his iPad. He's browsing the house sales websites desperate for something new to come on. I make us a cup of coffee, when I bring it over he drops the iPad down with a sigh.

'If I can afford it, it's ghastly. If I love it, I can't afford it. Have you any idea what places in this building go for?'

I shake my head. 'I asked Martin and he said he's not aware of anything coming up. He also said he would be because there are only twelve flats in this block and everyone confides in him.'

'Shame. I do so love this outlook…' He grins. '…almost as much as I loved the outlook from the other side of the river.'

I laugh along with him.

He's staying the night and we don't discuss flat buying again, instead focussing on his business, a little about my painting and a lot about our families. We discuss previous boyfriends and I admit there have been no serious ones for me. He expresses surprise, feigns shock. He's had two, one ended when his lover died. He looks so sad, so forlorn that I don't like to ask what he died from in case it upsets him. I chat on about my parents, my brothers and their families, and of course, more about Angie. I tell him how close we've always been, how I'm the child that no one planned or expected.

'Hey, I'm glad you came along,' he says, cuddling into me. 'Do you mind if we turn in early, I have work in the morning?'

'Oh, of course.' It's barely nine-thirty and I was enjoying chatting with him. Then it dawns on me perhaps he doesn't want to just sleep.

But he turns out his bedside light and is snoring before I've even finished in the bathroom.

☯☯☯

'Hey, *min kärlek*, I have to go.'

I was sound asleep; outside it is still dark.

'Oh? Hi. I didn't realise.'

'Hey, I know. Sorry. I'm flying to Scotland this morning and I need to get changed so need to get back to my place first.'

'Okay. Would you like me to drive you?' I start to get out of bed.

'No, no. Uber waiting outside. I should be back tonight. Okay if I stay with you? I've started packing up the house ready for the move and it's horrendous now.' He grins.

How can I resist that grin? 'Absolutely.'

'I'll ring you later.' He leans down, kisses me softly on the lips, he tastes of toothpaste, I dread to think what I taste of. Then he's gone.

I hear nothing from him all day but, I reason, he's busy. By six pm I'm expecting a call or message but nothing comes. By eight pm, I'm getting concerned, but then if he's flown to Scotland and finished working late

– not that I know what his plans in Scotland were – then he could just be landing now.

I message him.

By nine pm he hasn't replied.

By ten pm I'm scanning the internet looking for reports of a plane crash. I've messaged and rung him so many times it's bordering on stalking.

By eleven pm I decide he's not coming. I don't understand what I did wrong that he should be ghosting me. I climb into bed, defeated, distressed, worried that something has happened to him and no one knows to inform me.

I lie in bed staring at the lights from the river making patterns on the ceiling. I'm just dosing off when the door phone rings.

It's the police, I think.

'Hello?'

'You've got a visitor.' The voice is rough and unfamiliar, another agency concierge.

'Right.' I shake myself to focus.

'Says his name is Perry something.'

'Send him up, now.'

I hover by my open front door watching the lift ascend; it seems to be on slow mode.

The lift stops, the doors open and for a few seconds nothing happens. Then Perry steps out, dragging his small wheelie case behind him. He looks exhausted, ashen-faced.

'Are you okay?' I ask, rushing towards him and taking the case. His hands are cold.

'I'm fine. I came straight here. Sorry it's so late.'

'I've been ringing and messaging.'

'Battery,' he says, rolling his eyes. 'Didn't even have my power bank with me. Sorry if I've worried you.'

‘As long as you’re okay now.’ I usher him into my flat.

‘Been a pig of a day,’ he says, heading straight for the kitchen and running himself a glass of water directly from the tap.

‘I have chilled mineral water in the fridge.’

‘I don’t care what it is,’ he says, gulping down the water in one go.

‘What happened?’

He shakes his head, refills the glass from the tap. ‘I’ve got such a bloody headache.’

I watch him as he gulps a second glass down, water trickling down the sides of his mouth.

‘Are you sure you’re okay?’

‘Yes, I’m fine. Really. On my way to the airport to catch the flight home and suddenly the taxi I’m in is broadsided by an HGV. We went flying across the lanes, hit the central reservation.’ He stops, his eyes staring off into the distance as though reliving the moment.

‘Were you injured?’

‘No, not me. I was lucky. Just shocked. Taxi driver died though.’

‘Oh my God.’

‘Yeah.’ He starts to cry and I step forward and hug him tight.

I could have lost him; it’s taken all these years to find him and I could have lost him just like that, just like that poor taxi driver.

‘Yeah, so been with the paramedics, then the police wanted a statement, then I missed my plane and had to get on another.’ He mumbles all this into my chest as I hug him tighter.

☯☯☯

We both toss and turn before finally succumbing to sleep. As a consequence, we sleep in. I wake just after nine and slide out of bed as quietly as possible, have a quick shower, dress and watch my sleeping lover. After I've made coffee and eaten toast I check on him again. It's almost ten and his eyes are still shut. I turn to leave.

'Hey, Adam, what time is it?'

'Nearly ten.'

He sits up slowly and looks around the room, frowning as he gets his bearings. He looks confused, then shakes his head.

'You're not working today, are you? Only I've let you sleep on. I thought you could do with it.'

'No work. I need to visit my mother later, but no work, thank God.'

'I've made coffee, would you like some?'

'I would. Maybe I'll take it in the bath. I feel the need for a good soak.'

I smile. 'You go ahead, I'll bring your coffee in.'

He's laying back, his eyes closed, when I take his coffee in. I pull up a little stool and put the cup down. He opens his eyes.

'I've put your phone on to charge.'

'Shit, I forgot about that last night. I bet it's full of messages.'

'Mostly mine. Probably.'

'Have you checked?' He sits up slightly.

'Of course not. Anyway, it's switched itself off.'

'Oh yes.' He lies back down in the bath.

'How are you feeling now?'

'Okay. I guess. I can't get the image of that poor man out of my head. Blood everywhere.' He shakes his head, wipes his eyes with the back of his hands.

'Would you like me to wash your hair?' I ask, hoping

to distract him.

'Hey, yeah, that would be good. Very good.'

I'm just finishing the final rinse – his hair requires such a lot of conditioner – when we're both surprised by a voice calling out.

'What the f….?' Perry says, looking alarmed.

'It's Jasper.' I dry my hands and call out to him. 'Coming.'

'Don't let him in here,' Perry says.

'Don't worry, I won't.'

'I don't want to meet him either, not today. I'm really not in the right frame of mind to be jolly with people.'

I nod. A little part of me feels elated that he doesn't class me as *people.* I feel so comfortable with Perry, as though we've known each other for years and I think he's feeling the same way. I'm desperately sad about the taxi driver but in a way I think what's happened has brought us closer. I close the bathroom door firmly behind me.

Jasper is helping himself to coffee when I come through from the bathroom.

'Adam, darling, I have another commission for you.'

'Great, thank you.'

'You might look more pleased.'

'Sorry, just…'

He tilts his head waiting for me to elaborate.

'Just stuff going on,' I say, not wanting to share any more with him.

'Oh, have I disturbed you. Is your lover here?'

I don't like the way he says lover.

'Can I meet him?'

'No. He's in the bath, he'll be a while.'

'I can wait.'

'Now's not a good time. Bring your coffee into the studio and you can brief me in there.'

Jasper spends half an hour telling me about the commission. It involves a meeting with the client, something I've always enjoyed. Finally, we venture out of the studio and I half expect Perry to be waiting for me, but there's no sign of him.

'Oh,' says Jasper, obviously expecting to see Perry too.

I don't invite him to sit down, I don't offer him another coffee. 'Email me the details and I'll arrange a client visit,' I tell him.

'Will do, dear boy. I'll probably come with you.'

I consider this for a moment or two. 'Okay.' It's not as though it's unusual, he has often come to visit clients with me.

'Oh, I almost forgot,' he says, stalling near the front door. 'Gerard was so delighted with how your show went that he's keen to do another. Is three months long enough for you to produce enough to fill his gallery? We have a few bits left from last time, they can go back in. If you want to go ahead he's happy to store what he's got off site with his other stuff.'

'He can't just keep it for sale in his gallery?'

'No, he doesn't do that, he only has shows for specific artists. I thought you understood that.'

'Yes, sorry. Of course. I've got some ideas. Amsterdam quite inspired me.'

'Excellent.' He hugs me and finally leaves.

I close the door behind him and lean on it.

Perry appears in the bedroom corridor hallway.

'I'm sorry that took so long,' I say. 'You should have come out and met him, I think he's desperate to meet you.'

Perry shakes his head slowly. 'Not really in the mood today. Anyway, I've been catching up on my emails and messages.'

'Breakfast?' I ask him.

He nods slowly.

'Hey,' he says, sounding tentative. 'Your friend, Jasper, he walks in here all the time like that?'

'I suppose. Would you like cereal and toast, or eggs maybe?'

'Sure.' He frowns. 'If you hadn't called out to him would he have wandered around looking for you.'

I ponder this for a second too long. I don't know where Jasper wanders looking for me if I'm not here. I've never thought about it before. I trust Jasper implicitly.

'Maybe.'

'Yeah, that's what I thought. He could walk in on us in bed. We could be, you know… I said we needed to sort out your security and the first thing we need to do is get your lock changed and speak to the guys downstairs, no one should just be waltzing in unannounced. I worry about you, *min kärlek*. And after yesterday I worry more.'

'I'm fine. After yesterday I'm more worried about you.' I pull eggs from the fridge. 'Scrambled okay?'

He nods. 'You need to tell Jasper he can't do that any longer. After I've eaten, I'll call a locksmith. This open house nonsense has to stop.'

Thirteen

It costs over two hundred pounds to get the lock changed and upgraded. Perry insists on paying. The two guys who do it talk constantly about deadlocks and deadbolts. I've always felt safe here so am finding it all a bit over the top especially when they say that these keys cannot be replicated, if I lose them – then it's a new lock again. After they've gone Perry locks the door from the inside.

'I feel a lot happier now I know you're secure. Here's the keys.' He hands me a ring of three keys.

'Would *you* like one?' I ask, almost doing a poochy poo face at him before I remember I'm not with Angie.

'Would you like me to have one?' His face is deadly serious.

'I think I would.' I pull a key off the ring and hand it over.

'What about the other one, the spare? You're not going to give it to Jasper, are you?' Although it's a question it feels more like an order.

'No, not if you think I shouldn't. But I'd like Angie to have one.'

'I don't think that's a good idea either.'

'But she's my sister.'

'Hey, yeah, I get that. But what if someone steals it from her?'

'Unlikely.' I laugh.

'Adam, when I met you I didn't know that you were this famous painter, but now I do, I really worry for your security. Promise me you won't give her a new key.' He waits.

'Okay, I don't suppose she needs it anyway, I'm usually here when she arrives and she invariably forgets hers. By the way, she's coming up at the weekend. She's looking forward to meeting you.'

He doesn't respond, instead suggesting that we go down and speak to the concierge right now. On the way down in the lift he briefs me on what to say, everyone is to be announced and no one is to come up unless I okay it. And if I'm not in, no one is allowed up. I point out that since no one has a key that would be pretty pointless.

I'm sorry to see that Martin isn't on duty today, instead it's an agency concierge I've not seen before. I explain the new arrangements while Perry hovers in the background. The concierge nods over at Perry.

'Oh, that doesn't apply to Perry. He'll be here often.'

'Will sir be needing a fob for the car park?' he asks Perry.

It hadn't even occurred to me but before I even have time to consider it, Perry says that yes, he would.

'I'll order that in, sir. It should be ready for you tomorrow. I'll get it delivered up to your apartment.'

'You don't have a car,' I say to Perry in the lift on way back up.

'I do. It's in the garage at the back of my house. I just don't use it very often; taxis and the underground are quicker. But if I'm moving out of my house I may need to bring it here short term. That would be okay, wouldn't it?'

'Sure, I'm allocated two spaces down there. How quickly do you expect to move out?'

'I don't know. Soon. The buyers are really pushing. I think they want to exchange and complete on the same day. That's why I need to find somewhere else *snabbt*. There was a message left on my phone yesterday about a place in Kensington. We could go look this afternoon.'

'I thought you were visiting your mum today.' I'm sure that's what he said earlier.

'Hey, yeah, I was. But I rang the rehabilitation home and they put me through to her. She doesn't really do mobile phones but isn't too bad on a landline. We had a nice chat. Or rather, I chatted and she grunted her answers, which is a definite improvement. So I don't feel the need to rush over there just yet.'

☯☯☯

The flat in Kensington is in a mansion block. It's small compared to mine, is top floor, has sweeping views over the rooftops but no balcony.

'I can live without that,' Perry says, when I mention it. 'I can pop round and use yours.' He grins. 'Let's face it, nothing compares to yours. This place may be top floor but it's not a penthouse, is it?'

'No, I suppose not.'

'Hey, I could definitely live here,' he says, making sure we are out of earshot of the agent.

'It is a great property.' It is. It's been fully renovated, has a new kitchen and bathrooms.

'I'll let you know,' he says to the agent. 'I need to give it some thought.'

The agent, smelling a sale, smiles. 'Don't wait too

long, properties in this block don't come up very often and they don't hang around.'

'I love it,' he tells me once we're in my car. 'I'm going to put an offer in. My place is sold so I'm a good buyer.'

'It's great. I'm delighted for you.' I really am, I can imagine visiting him there, staying the night. 'It's very handy for *Harrods*.'

He laughs. 'Adam, only you could say that.'

On the way home Perry suggests we get some ingredients in so he can cook us both a meal, apparently cooking is one of his hobbies. We stop off at a deli not far from my place and stock up. I insist on paying. It's the first time I've paid for anything.

The meal he cooks is amazing, although it's not what I expected. I was anticipating something Swedish but when I say this to Perry he laughs.

'You must be joking. It's all dried fish and pickled things. That's what my *mormor* used to feed me as a kid. Horrible.' He laughs. 'I have a very British palate curtesy of my mother.'

That would explain his choice of restaurants while we were in Stockholm. Minimum Swedish fare on the menu.

'I suppose I should tell Jasper his key won't work any longer.' I'm thinking aloud.

Perry shrugs. 'He'll find out easily enough the next time he visits. I wouldn't bother telling him.'

☯☯☯

The next couple of days fly by and Perry cooks for us again, which is just as well since I need to work. He doesn't bother me while I'm in my studio which is very considerate of him. When I ask what he's been doing, apart for cooking for me, he laughs and says work.

Although he has cancelled all meetings for this week. He says he's fine now but I think he's still traumatised by the taxi accident.

'Will you have to go to the inquest, or something, give evidence?' I ask him over dinner on Thursday evening. He's cooked meatballs as an homage to his half-homeland, though he says he doesn't particularly like them and thinks *IKEA's* are better. I, on the other hand, think they're great.

'I hope not.' He shudders. 'I've no desire to relive that in a hurry.'

'No, of course not.' I'm sorry I brought it up now.

'Hey,' he says, after clearing the table and putting an elaborate fruit and cream pudding in front of me.

'Wow, is this some special Swedish pudding.'

He laughs. 'No, it's fruit and cream, you had some strawberries approaching their sell by date in the fridge so I thought I'd use them up.'

I join in his laughter. I love being with him, it's just so easy, so comfortable.

'Hey,' he starts again. 'I was thinking…'

'Yeah?'

'How great it's been. How healing it's been for me to be here with you.'

I reach over and grip his hand. I've enjoyed every minute of it too. In fact, I'm really close to asking him to move in, except I know it's too soon. 'Yeah,' I agree with him.

'So, I was wondering if you might put your sister off this weekend, just so we can have a bit more time alone, just the two of us. I have to go back to work on Monday, I have a meeting in Stockholm but I'm going to try and do there and back in a day.'

'Can you do that?'

'Ja, early start, late finish, but no overnight. Can I stay here on Monday night?'

'Of course you can.'

'So, what about your sister?'

I don't want to put Angie off. I haven't seen her in a while, but on the other hand, I'm sure she'll understand. 'Yeah, I'll ring her later.'

I go into my studio to ring Angie, I don't want Perry to hear what I say but, moreover, I don't want him to hear her reaction.

'How is your sister?' Perry asks later, when we're in bed.

'Yeah, she's good. She understands why coming up this weekend wouldn't be a good idea.'

'She understands?'

'Yeah. I had to explain the situation to her.'

'You told her about the accident?'

'I had to. It was only fair.'

He's silent for a moment or two and I feel the tension in the air. 'Ja, I guess,' he says.

'Sorry, I know you don't want to be reminded.'

'Do you tell your sister everything?'

'Pretty much. We are very close.'

'I mean everything? Us? This.' He strokes my face then lets his hand wander down my body.

'Of course not. She's my *sister*.'

He laughs lightly, turns over and goes to sleep.

☯☯☯

We've had a lovely weekend, we didn't do anything except chill, watch TV – it seems Perry has a penchant for romcoms – and eat. We don't drink a massive amount, certainly not the quantity of wine that Angie and

I would have worked our way through in a weekend. I've even done some work. This afternoon we went for a walk in the park and it suddenly started to rain. We ran for cover while the heavens opened, huddled together, rain dripping off the end of our noses. Oddly, it felt romantic. Perry commented on it too. Said it reminded him of *Pride and Prejudice*, the Keira Knightly version.

Now it's Sunday evening and I'm sorry he'll be away all day tomorrow but I'm going on the client visit with Jasper so that will distract me.

'Hey, he says. 'Did I tell you I rang the agent? I made an offer.'

'No, when?'

'When you were working yesterday.'

'And?'

'She couldn't get hold of the owner, so…' He wiggles his head from side to side. 'Hopefully I'll hear something tomorrow.'

'I'll keep my fingers crossed for you.' A part of me is sorry. Maybe I should suggest he moves in here with me. Is it really too soon?

☯☯☯

'Hey,' he says, waking me.

'What time is it?'

'Just after five. No need for you to get up. Just wanted to let you know I'm off.'

'Take extra care of yourself.' This feels strangely familiar and I shudder at the thought that something might happen to him. Again. That he might not be so lucky a second time.

'Hey, don't worry. Lightning never strikes twice.' Then he's gone leaving me wide awake and concerned.

I know that statistically he's correct, but it doesn't stop me from worrying all day.

It's just after seven when he bursts through the door. He's carrying flowers. He thrusts them at me. I'm quite overwhelmed. No one has ever bought me flowers. No one. Ever.

'Thank you, they're amazing.'

He shrugs, smiles and leans in for a hug while I'm still clutching the flowers.

'I have to confess I picked them up at the airport. I just thought they would cheer you up.'

'Did I look that bad this morning?'

'You looked a bit glum. What's that I can smell?'

'It's an oven ready meal. I've told you before I'm no cook, I only have one dish really and I'm lazy. It won't be ready for a while; I didn't know when you'd be back.'

'It still smells good.' He takes of his coat, dumps it on the sofa. How easily he fits in here. I should just ask him to move in.

'Did it go okay today?' What I mean is, did he not have an accident.

'Yeah, fine. No crashes.' He half grins then corrects himself. 'Sorry, that was in bad taste considering what happened.'

'As long as you're okay.'

I wander off to find something to put the flowers in, vases not being something I've ever had a lot of use for. There is, however, something suitable on the hall table, I think Angie may have bought it as a house warming present. I rinse it out and plonk the flowers in it, then put them in the middle of the dining table.

'Hey,' Perry calls. 'I had a call from the estate agent today. Well two calls from two estate agents.'

'Oh?'

'Yeah, my buyers want to really speed things up. They want to complete next Tuesday.'

'Can you do that?'

'Yes, I can clear everything out by then, no problem. I've no more meetings this week, just routine stuff, so I can. The legals are okay on my side, so it's up to them.'

'I can help clear out your place.'

He glances at me, smiles then shakes his head. 'No, you can't. You have to work.'

I'm relieved since boxing up other people's crap isn't my idea of fun, no matter how much I like them. Also, I'm on a roll with my work, feeling inspired and creative and I don't want to lose that.

'What about the other agent?'

A smile that spreads across his face lights up his eyes making the skin underneath crinkle. 'The seller has accepted my offer.'

'Yes. This calls for champagne,' I say, though I feel slightly deflated. I open the fridge, pull one out; I always keep a bottle just in case. Angie's idea long ago and it's surprising how often the bottles are drunk.

'Yes and no. They want to complete quickly, which is fine by me, but they've had another offer slightly higher than mine. They'll only take it off the market if I pay the deposit now. This week. They're only going with me because I'm effectively a cash buyer, or I will be next week.'

'Oh. How much is the deposit?'

'Ten per cent.' He picks up the champagne bottle and pops the cork.

'But that's… how much?' I'm trying to remember what the asking price was.

'Seventy-five thousand pounds,' he says, just as the champagne dribbles out of the top of the bottle. He grabs the glasses and begins to pour.

'So…' I don't know what to say. 'You have that money?'

'No, of course not. I plough all my spare cash into the business, though it does pay off. I'll have enough to pay for the place outright next week, but in the meantime, I've spoken to my moneyman and he's arranging a bridging loan.'

'Aren't they expensive?' After I've said it I wish I hadn't.

'Yeah,' he says. 'Interest is high on such loans. But it's only for a short time. I'm pressuring my solicitor to get on with buying it. Six weeks max I hope.'

Fourteen

'I've got a big favour to ask you,' Perry says over breakfast the next morning. He's made us scrambled eggs and smoked salmon, having first popped out to the deli to pick up supplies.

'Yeah?'

'As you know my buyers get the house next week and I have to clear it out.'

I nod my agreement.

'Well, once done I'll be homeless.' He pauses for a second or two before continuing. 'I was wondering if I could stay with you until I get possession of the Kensington flat?'

'Absolutely, of course. I'd assumed you would.' I had, and I'm thrilled.

'Are you sure? Only say if you're not, I don't want to impose on you. We've only been together a short while, even though, for me, it feels as though I've known you forever.'

'Me too.'

He leans over and kisses me. '*Min kärlek*,' he says. 'Thank you so much.' He stands up. 'I'm just going to clear this away then I must be off. Boxes to pack, furniture to arrange storage for, though not much, and I need to ring a charity organisation that takes furniture. Just because I don't want it doesn't mean someone else won't love it.' He grimaces and it makes me laugh as he starts to load the dishwasher. 'I'll probably bring my car back here tonight too.'

'You know where to park, and you have the car park fob.'

'I do, and the number for the rear door. I'm so excited to be moving. It seems to have dragged on for ages and now suddenly it's all coming together.'

After he's gone I head off to my studio and have a very productive day.

Perry comes back about six, he's carrying a couple of bags with him.

'Clothes,' he says. 'I hope you don't mind.'

'Of course not. Here…' I take a bag from him and together we head towards my bedroom. There is plenty of space in the wardrobes, since I'm not a big clothes lover, and we soon have his items put away. 'How did it go with your bridging loan?'

'No problems. Should be through by Thursday which is good because I have to put that deposit down by Friday. So, all good. Have you had a good day?'

'I have.'

Perry spends the next few days clearing his old house out and visiting his mother while I spend my time painting. That trip to Amsterdam has inspired me so much. By Friday I'm getting on so well and am deep in concentration when the door phone buzzes.

'It's me,' Jasper says, when I answer.

'Oh hello. Come on up.'

'I got stopped by your man.'

'Oh, yes, sorry. New regime. Meant to tell you.' I didn't, but if it helps Jasper accept the change, that's fine.

When he arrives I'm waiting with the front door open. He has his key in his hand. He looks annoyed.

'Your man downstairs says that this key won't work any longer. Says you've changed the locks. Is that right?'

'Oh, yes.' I smile and usher him into the flat.

'Do I get another key then?'

'No, I'm not giving them out. Security and stuff, you know,' I add, vaguely, turning away.

'Has something happened, dear boy? Have you been burgled? Heaven forbid.'

'No, no. Just tightening up on security in general. You can't be too careful, can you?'

'So I have to go through your man downstairs every time? He didn't want to give me the phone you know, he wanted to speak to you himself. Announce me.' He shudders.

I smile and offer him a cup of tea and hope that will distract him, but just to make sure, while the tea is brewing I take him through to the studio and show him my progress.

'Oh, my.' He sits down in the armchair I keep in there, and sighs deeply. 'I think these are your best work. Stunning, quite stunning.'

'Thank you.'

'Is this the commissioned piece? It's fantastic and almost finished?'

'Yes. The others are for the gallery show.'

'Gerard will be so pleased. Can I take a few shots to send him?' He pulls out his phone and clicks away before I even agree he can.

He stays for over an hour and when he announces he's leaving I'm relieved that the new lock situation hasn't been mentioned again. I escort him to the lift and give him a goodbye hug and that's when he says it.

'Was it his idea to change the locks?'

'Who, Martin?' I know I'm being disingenuous.

'Martin? I thought his name was Perry.'

'Martin is the concierge downstairs.' Deliberate misdirection but I suspect it won't work on Jasper, he's far too wily.

'I know who Martin is, I've been coming here long enough, darling. Incidentally, Martin's on holiday today. I meant Perry. Has he moved in yet?'

I hadn't realised how old and mean Jasper is looking these days.

'No, I lie. It was my idea.' I don't answer his last question.

☯☯☯

Perry arrives just before four pm, he's grinning like a maniac.

'Okay?' I ask, keen to know what's made him so happy.

'Better than okay. Money's gone through, deposit is down on the Kensington flat and there's no turning back now.'

'Does this call for more champagne?'

'Oh I think so. Also, my house is officially empty. A charity van arrived today and took everything I didn't want, they nearly bit my hand off after being a bit standoffish on the phone saying they'd need to inspect everything.' He shrugs. 'I'm beginning to wonder if I could have sold some of it.'

'Did they take everything?' I'm hoping the bed has gone but also wondering what he will put in his new flat.

'No, I've had a few bits put into storage. Oh happy days.' He grabs me and waltzes me around the room before we fall clumsily in a heap onto the sofa.

His phone rings and he pulls it out of his pocket and answers. He jumps up, mouths, 'Agent,' at me, then wanders off into our bedroom – that's how I'm already thinking of it, *our* bedroom – to continue the call.

A few minutes later, just as I'm lining up the champagne and glasses on the kitchen island, he's back.

'Don't open that,' he says, his face glum.

'What's happened?'

'Fucking buyers have pulled out.'

I've never heard him swear before.

'What? But they were so keen.'

'Yep, they were the ones pushing and pushing and now pffft, they don't want it.'

'But why?'

'I don't know. Didn't say. Of course it's cost them next to nothing other than solicitor fees. It's costing me a bloody fortune in bridging loan interest. Bastards.' He looks as though he might cry.

'I'm so sorry.' I wrap my arms around him, hug him tight. He just hangs there limply. 'What can we do?'

'Agent is putting it back on the market as we speak. Says he might be able to get more for it.' He pulls away from me. 'He thinks now it's empty it might be more attractive.'

'Really? Do you think that?'

'Fingers crossed he's right. He has viewings lined up for tomorrow. Not that it helps with my bridging loan interest.' He slumps onto the sofa looking totally downhearted.

We spend a very quiet weekend together. Ironically, Angie isn't coming up this weekend because she has a wedding to go to. It's probably just as well, I don't think Perry is in the mood for mixing with anyone other than me.

We're having a subdued breakfast on Monday morning before I start work and he goes to visit his mum, when his phone rings.

'Agent,' he says, getting up from the table and taking the call in our bedroom again.

When he comes back he looks concerned.

'Well?'

'Yeah, had an offer. It is actually better than the previous one, so that's something.' He pulls his mouth down at the corners.

'That's good, isn't it?'

'Ja, but they haven't sold their place yet. So, chain and waiting. I'm just so pissed off with the original buyers.'

'What are you going to do?'

'I've told the agent to accept the offer but keep the place on the market. Maybe I'll get an offer from someone who's proceedable.' He sighs, glances at his watch, an expensive looking piece that I've never seen before.

'New watch?' I ask.

He glances back down at it. 'Oh, no, it was in the house, in a drawer. Quite forgot I had it, thought I might as well wear it.'

'Nice.'

'I need to get off. See how Mum is doing.' He comes over and kisses me goodbye, then he's gone and I am about to go into my studio when I glance around the place. It looks very untidy in here after our quiet weekend and my cleaner doesn't come until later in the week, so I spend an hour tidying and cleaning. I even change the bed because it smells far from fresh after the two of us have slept in it.

The week drags on, Perry is home a lot and moping

around the place and generally feeling sorry for himself. He's had no more offers and it's making him very miserable, and short-tempered.

Angie has asked if she can come up this weekend and I've put her off. The last thing I want is for her to meet Perry when he's Mr Grumpy. She's disappointed.

On Monday Perry goes away on business for a few days and I have to admit that I'm almost relieved. Much as I love him, I find his mood since his house sale fell through hard to cope with. I suppose this is what it is like living with someone; give and take. I've lived alone for so long I've quite forgotten. The last time I lived with anyone was when I was at home fighting with my brothers and siding with my sister. And that was a long time ago.

On Thursday evening Perry announces that we're going away for the weekend, his treat. I tell him that he really doesn't have to treat me and I can pay for us, but he won't hear of it. He's already booked the flights, he tells me. We're going to Edinburgh.

When I ask why Edinburgh, assuming he has business there, he just says that it's a great city and we both need a break, him to forget about his house woes and me to recover from his moods. He says he knows he's moody and apologises profusely. I think I love him more than ever for that.

Of course I've had to put Angie off yet again, although I did hint that she could come on her own, she declined, saying that her main purpose for coming is to see me.

'Just as well she said no,' Perry says, having overheard my call. 'Since her key doesn't work any longer. Have you told her you've changed the locks?'

I have to admit, I haven't.

The flight from London to Edinburgh doesn't take long, of course we fly business class which seems excessive even to me for such a short journey. The hotel is five star and Perry has booked a suite. I'm concerned about how he's funding this given his bridging loan situation but he tells me not to worry.

We dine that evening in one of the hotel's private dining rooms, just the two of us. There's champagne and flowers and music playing. The food is, as expected, exquisite and we've had a few glasses of wine each. Perry says he doesn't want to open the champagne until after dinner. We've just finished the final course, and I must admit I am full to the brim, when suddenly the music is turned up and Perry rises from his seat. I wonder if he is going to ask me to dance. I might need some of that champagne if that's the case.

Then he drops to one knee in front of me, pulls out a little box and looks into my eyes, tears forming in his own.

'Adam,' he says, his voice hoarse. 'I can't tell you how much I love you, there's never been anyone like you for me. Will you marry me?'

Fifteen

The ring is platinum with a diamond in the middle. The style is simple and elegant, the shape just like a wedding ring.

For a moment or two I'm speechless. Stunned. I wasn't expecting this. Then it hits me, elation.

'Yes, yes, yes,' I stutter.

Perry grins, he looks relieved. 'I know it's been a whirlwind,' he says, putting the ring onto my finger. 'But I can't imagine not spending the rest of our lives together. It's us, together forever.'

'Me too,' I say, standing up, leaning down and pulling Perry up into my arms.

''Champagne?' he asks as he hugs me tightly.

The rest of the evening is a wonderful blur and when we wake in the morning we're both still grinning.

We do the sights in Edinburgh, the tourist stuff. I take photos, I even manage a few selfies with us both in them. Perry declares that he does not take a good photo.

'Is that why you don't have one of yourself on your website?' I ask.

He grins. 'You've got it in one,' he says, shooting his fingers at me.

'But I don't understand, I think you're stunning. I

think you're photogenic too, here look.' I show him a photo I've taken that he wasn't aware of, a side profile.

He shudders and pushes the phone away.

'I think you need therapy for that,' I say, laughing and hugging him. 'You're beautiful.'

'You're beautiful, Adam. I am not.'

'Definitely going to get you some therapy when we get home.'

He shakes his head and laughs. 'No thanks.'

☯☯☯

I wait until we're home on Sunday evening before video calling Angie. I don't go and hide in another room and Perry is busy making coffee in the background while I talk to her.

'You what?' she screeches.

'Perry asked me to marry him.'

'I thought that's what you said. That's quick, Adam. Did you say yes?'

'Of course I did.' Why would she think I would say anything else?

'I can hear clattering, is he there?'

'Yes.'

'Show me, show me. Put him on.'

'She wants to talk to you,' I call over to Perry.

He stays where he is, messing about with the coffee machine, clattering the cups. He waves over from his position. 'Hi Angie,' he calls, then turns away hunting the cupboards for biscuits.

'I can't see him properly, tell him to come closer.'

'I need to go to somewhere,' Perry says cryptically, disappearing out of sight.

'Where's he gone?'

'Toilet, I think.'

'Do I make him nervous,' she asks, laughing a little.

'I think you might.' I laugh a lot. 'Come up and meet him at the weekend.'

'Promise you won't bin me off again like you keep doing?' she asks, sounding petulant.

'I promise. Come Saturday, like normal. Let me know what time the train gets in and I'll pick you up from Paddington. I'm really looking forward to you two meeting.'

'Me too,' she says. 'It'll be nice to see him in person. Is his hair really that blond?'

'Oh yes. He's half Swedish.'

'I know, but…'

'But what?'

'Well not all Swedes are *that* blond, are they?'

'I suppose not but mine is.'

☯☯☯

Despite our engagement Perry is still depressed about his house sale falling through. He goes to visit his mum and he attends a couple of business meetings and he spends a lot of time on his laptop but, in general, he's very quiet. I can't stand to see him so miserable.

'I love my ring,' I tell him.

He smiles.

'But you don't have one.'

He shrugs.

'Why don't we go and choose one for you?'

'Hey, there's no need.'

'I think there is.'

'I'm not really a ring person,' he says, grimacing slightly. 'Watches, maybe, but not rings.'

'Would you like a watch then?' I'm sort of disappointed but happy to buy him a watch if that's what he'd like. I also hope that a little treat will cheer him up.

'Not really. I probably have enough.'

That's the end of that idea, then.

'Have you heard any more from your new buyers?'

'Yes, they're still very keen. But they still haven't sold their own house yet. The agent let slip this morning that it's only just gone on the market, like after they put an offer in on mine. Really, people shouldn't be out house shopping if they haven't sold their own or, at least, have it up for sale and are actively marketing it.' He shakes his head in despair. 'And the agent from the Kensington flat rang and asked for a status update. The seller is getting twitchy. He only let me have it because I could proceed so quickly. He's had an increased offer from that other party.'

'But you've paid the deposit.'

'Ja.' He sighs.

'Well he can't do anything other than wait, can he? He'd have to return your deposit.'

Perry gives me a sideways look before looking down at his feet. His shoulders go down too. Then he takes a great gulp of air.

'Perry?'

He turns away from me, but I don't let that stop me from grabbing hold of his shoulders and pulling him around.

'What's wrong? Tell me.' Now I'm really worried about him.

'Adam, I've done the most stupid thing. The most stupid.'

'It can't be that bad. Tell me and it might not be so bad. You know, a trouble shared and all that…'

'The deposit is non-refundable.'

'No, that's not right. You'll get it back if he doesn't proceed with the sale, won't you?'

He shakes his head, tears well up in his eyes. 'I won't. I signed the contract. We've exchanged. I felt so sure everything would be fine. My house was sold, it was days away from completing…' He throws himself at me and I hug him.

'I know, I know. But you can still buy the flat.'

'I can't.'

'You can. Your house will sell. Okay it may take a little longer than the original plan…'

'No, no,' he interrupts. 'There was a clause, a deadline. If I don't complete by then I lose my deposit.'

'Is that right. I mean, is that even legal?' It sounds very dodgy to me.

'Yes, I'm afraid it is. My solicitor has been working on it, trying to extend the deadline, but the seller's not budging. At the moment my solicitor is doing all the conveyancing stuff as fast as he can so that when the money does come through I'm ready to go immediately, but we're nowhere near that yet. What am I going to do?'

'Can't you borrow more, increase the bridging loan until your house sells?'

He shakes his head. 'No, I'm basically maxed out. What with Mum's rehabilitation fees… I wouldn't care but with what I'll get from the house sale I'll only have a tiny mortgage.' He lets out a bitter laugh.

'Surely your lender can help?' Although I thought he said he had enough to pay for it outright.

'No. I've tried. Now they're even getting twitchy about the bridging loan. By pushing them I may have made my situation worse.'

'When's the deadline?'

He pulls away from me. His eyes red-rimmed, his face grey, even his hair looks grey. 'Two weeks,' he says, taking another gulp of air. 'In two weeks I lose seventy-five thousand pounds and I'll have nothing to show for it other than a high interest debt. Maybe I should just give up and move back into the house, not sell it. Cut my losses.'

'You've got rid of all the furniture,' I quip, trying to lighten the mood, though God knows how my misplaced comment will help.

A glint sparks in his eye. 'Not all of it. I still have the bed. You can still visit me.'

I try not to laugh. Then he grins. At least he does still have a sense of humour.

Neither of us sleeps very well. We lie awake together but separate. I feel desperately sorry for Perry. How can this have happened? How can he have been so naïve. I know he thought it was a sure thing, it *was* a sure thing, but to sign a contract with such a deadline, especially with such a large deposit. I'm horrified for him. And upset. If only there was something I could do to help.

☯☯☯

It's Friday morning and the idea comes to me in the shower. I rinse the shampoo off my hair as fast as I can so that I can tell Perry. I really don't know why this didn't occur to me before.

He's still in bed, sitting up, flicking through his phone, his face glum.

'Why don't I lend you the balance?' I flop down on the bed not caring that I might soak the bedding with my damp towels, something I know annoys Perry. He glances quickly at the towels but doesn't mention them.

'What?' he says, dropping his phone and screwing up his face. 'What are you saying?'

'Why don't I lend you the money?'

'You can't.'

'Why not? We're getting married. What's yours will be mine and what's mine will be yours. What's the difference?' I feel rather proud of my argument.

'Do you have a spare three-quarters of a million hanging around then?' He shakes his head as though I'm a daft child.

'Of course not. But I do have substantial investments and I can take out a mortgage on this place for the balance.'

'I couldn't let you do that.'

'I'm doing it.' I'm taking charge.

'No.' He shakes his head and turns to look out of the window, stare at the river.

'I'm going to. I'll talk to my financial advisor today to get the cash from my investments and I'll see about a mortgage. I own this place outright so it should be easy. I'm a good bet.'

Perry stares at me. Tears are running down his face. He opens his mouth to speak but a great howl comes out. I hug him. We stay like that for minutes. Eventually he pulls away.

'You'd do that, for me?'

'Yes. Absolutely.'

He shakes his head in disbelief then grins at me. '*Min kärlek*.'

The rest of the day goes by in a blur and by the end the wheels are in motion. My financial advisor isn't very happy, says I'm going to lose interest by cashing in my investments so suddenly – what he means is that he will lose commission. I tell him I don't care. This is far more important. He agrees to arrange a mortgage and starts to shop around for the best deal for me.

'At the very least you need to get your name on the deeds of that flat,' he says, his parting shot before I end the call. I have no intention of doing that, why should I? When we're married, everything will be joint.

Perry is happy with me. Delighted. He's been hyper excited and anxious all day. As have I. He's been out to the deli again and bought food to cook. I don't want to tell him that I can hardly taste it.

'You haven't done any work today,' he says, as he's clearing our plates away.

'I beg to differ,' I say, with a laugh.

'No, proper work. Your work. The work you love, your art.'

'No, well…' I shrug.

'Why don't you go and get a few hours in now?'

'Do you mind? Only I thought you liked us to spend the evenings together when you're here.'

'Of course I do. But you've spent all day doing this amazing thing for me. Please, go and do something you love.' He grins. 'Anyway, you need to earn money, you'll have a mortgage to pay soon.' He laughs. I laugh. Then he frowns. 'How is it that you don't already have a mortgage on this place? It must have cost a fortune.'

'I bought it a long time ago. It was cheaper then than it would be now, obviously. I did have a mortgage but whenever I had a bit of a windfall from selling my work, I paid a big chunk off the mortgage. I've been mortgage free for about five years now.'

'Wow. That's my goal. If the business continues to do well…'

'It will,' I assure him. 'It will.'

We both sleep well that night.

Saturday morning and I wake up to find Perry is no longer in bed with me. I can hear the shower running and I briefly consider joining him. Then the showers stops so I flop back against the pillows and wait for him to come out of the bathroom. I've had another brilliant idea.

'Hey,' he says, as he comes out. 'Sleep well?'

'I did, I did. I've had an idea.'

He eyes me suspiciously. 'Another one? I hope it's as good as the last, ja?'

'Ja,' I say, mimicking him. 'I've been thinking. Why don't you move in here? Permanently.'

'Ja? But what about the Kensington flat?'

'Rent it out. It can provide you with a nice income to plough back into your business, or pay off your mortgage quicker, or whatever.'

He tips his head from one side to the other. 'Hey, yeah. That's a good idea.'

'I know. I'm full of them lately.' Now it's my turn to grin. 'It's not as though we'll be living separately once we're married, is it?'

'No, of course not.'

'And about that,' I add. 'We should start looking at dates. I don't want to wait too long.'

'No,' he says, dropping down onto the bed and hugging me. 'Me neither. Now get up and showered and dressed because I'm looking forward to meeting this sister of yours today.' With that he yanks the covers from the bed and slaps my thigh.

When I come out of the bathroom Perry is sitting on the bed fully dressed, his phone in his hand. He looks glum. Again.

'What's wrong? Not the flat again. You can't be

gazumped yet.'

He shakes his head slowly then looks at me. 'It's my mum. She's had another stroke.'

I drop down on the bed next to him, put my arm around his shoulder, pull him in close.

'When? Is she okay?' I hope I don't regret asking that.

'About an hour ago. They're taking her back to hospital; ambulance is there ready to go once she's stable enough to move. I need to go now. I'm so sorry, Adam, I won't get to meet your sister today.'

'Don't worry about that, you go. Go and get your mum better.' How crass and insensitive that sounds.

It seems if it's not one thing, it's another. I just wish I could sort out his mum as easily as I've sorted out his house problems.

Sixteen

Angie is, of course, disappointed not to meet Perry. Although she does later admit that she's quite pleased to have me all to herself.

We have the same kind of weekend together we've been having for years. It's as though nothing has changed but the reality is that everything has changed.

She's brought her yang stone and remembers to get it out of her bag this time and I hunt around for my yin.

'Here it is.' I pull it from the back of the drawer and place it down on the kitchen island next to hers.

'I don't know what happened to my googly eye,' she says, with a laugh as she shakes my stone to make the eye move.

'I don't know how mine has stayed on.'

'What shall we do with them?'

'Don't know,' I say, with a shrug. 'Have you an idea?' Truth is I haven't even thought about it and my phone rings before I can even try now. 'Ah, need to take this, it's Perry.' I rush off into our bedroom.

'How is he?' Angie asks when I come back. 'How's his mum.'

I shake my head. 'Really not looking good for his mum. You can imagine how devastated he is.'

'Poor Perry. Poor Perry's mum.' She sounds glib, almost uncaring. But what can anyone really say? I sounded the same when I was speaking to Perry just minutes ago. It's a shit situation.

Angie picks up the stones and scrutinises them. 'Did you know that we have these round the wrong way?'

'No? What do you mean?'

'Yin is black but feminine. Yang is white but male. You have the girly one,' she teases.

'And you have the butch one, sounds about right.'

She hurls the stones at me and I, rather deftly, catch them, one in each hand. 'I might keep them both.'

'No, give me back my yang. Actually, we do have them the right way round, I have you and you have me.' She snatches yang and clutches it to her chest. 'Although I've been replaced now.'

'You should be pleased for me. You wanted me to find a boyfriend.'

'Yeah, I did. Just not a fiancé yet.'

There's nothing I can say to that.

☯☯☯

Perry messages after I've dropped Angie at the station, he says he's going to stay another night. My heart drops, not just for him but, selfishly, for myself. I'm missing him like crazy. In an attempt to cheer him up I message him that Angie is coming up again next weekend to meet him.

He doesn't reply. I try not to read anything into that; he's probably just busy with his mum.

He actually doesn't return until Tuesday mid-afternoon. During his absence I have tried to concentrate on my painting. It's odd, before he came into my life I just worked, nothing seemed to get in the way. Now I am struggling to concentrate as I worry about his welfare and his mother's health.

Jasper pays me a call on Tuesday too. Fortunately, he doesn't mention the key situation again although he does appear nervous and on edge. He asks if Perry is about and when I say he's not he seems to relax.

In the studio he spends his time examining the finished pieces.

'This I love,' he says, pulling out his phone and taking a quick photo. 'Gerard will love it too. Probably make it the centrepiece. It's probably your best work ever. Stunning. What inspired you?' He turns and waits for my reply.

'Amsterdam,' I say, truthfully.

He nods. 'You've not done as much as I was expecting,' he says, inspecting my other pieces. He sounds bitchy. Has he always sounded like that or am I just noticing it now?

'No. There's been a lot going on.' I leave it there, I'm not about to start telling him about our finances or Perry's mum.

'So I see,' he says, nodding at my ring. 'When did that happen?'

In all the furore I'd almost forgotten that I hadn't really told anyone. Not Jasper, not Rue, not Brent, not any of my friends, not that I've seen any of them recently.

'Oh, yes. Perry asked me to marry him.' I've only told my family via text although Angie will have filled them in with any detail.

'So I hear.'

'Who from?'

'Angie.' He gives me such a smug smile I want to slap it off his face. Of course, I don't.

'I didn't know you were so friendly with Angie.'

He shrugs. 'You need to crack on,' he says, glancing around.

'I've got twelve pieces here.'

'And three of them aren't finished. And you know we need a minimum of eighteen to fill Gerard's gallery.'

'And the show is two months away. No problem,' I add, dismissively.

'Good. Where is he? Your…' he pauses. 'Fiancé.'

'Work.' I'm definitely not discussing anything with Jasper especially if he's in cahoots with Angie. I don't like that they are talking about me behind my back. They say that attack is the best form of defence so I turn the questions towards him. 'So how is Gerard? Are you two an item now?'

He gives me a withering look. 'Darling, Gerard and I have been many items over the years. I think you'd call us friends with benefits. I find it works very well. We both do. You should try it.'

'I don't need to.'

'No. Well. I'd better go so you can crack on. I'll be back next week, similar time probably, for a progress report.'

'You don't need to come round for that. I can call you. Or text.'

'I do need to see it for myself, dear boy. Gerard has refused Luke Pitney-Goddard, you know, *the* latest hot artist, for your show. So…' He turns on his heels and heads for the front door.

'That child,' I say, sounding far more bitchy than Jasper did earlier.

'You were that child once, darling. So you need to keep your art front and centre if you don't want to be overtaken by the new boy on the block.'

It's less than ten minutes after he's gone and I've barely picked up a paintbrush when Perry bursts in through the front door. I rush from my studio to see him.

He looks awful. Ashen faced, dark-eyed. I'm afraid to ask how she is but I don't have to.

'She's gone,' he says.

'I'm so sorry.' I rush to him, hold him, but it seems so inadequate. 'When?'

'Hour or so before I left. That's why I left. Can't do anything now, can I? Can't save her now.'

'No.'

'I've just come home to change, sleep in your wonderful bed and see you. I'll have to be off again in the morning. Arrange the funeral and sort everything out.' He shudders in my arms.

'Would you like me to come with you?'

'No, *min kärlek*, you need to work.' He pulls himself away from me and shrugs off his jacket.

'You sound like Jasper.' I sigh.

'He's been here?'

'Yes, earlier.'

'Ah. Did you tell him about us? How we're engaged?'

'I did. He said congratulations,' I lie.

'You didn't tell him about my mother, about our financial arrangements?' Perry looks horrified.

'Certainly not. Anyway, he was too busy nagging about me being ready for the show in Gerrard's gallery. He was quite nasty; I've never noticed it in the past.'

'Jealous. He thought you were his.'

'No. Maybe.'

Perry goes off to have a shower while I flick through my phone wondering what food we can order in at this time of day.

'Let's go out,' he says when I ask him. 'I need some

normality.' He forces a little smile. 'Get your coat, you've pulled.' It's sort of funny.

'This is so good,' Perry says, when we're sitting eating in the little café that Angie and I so love. 'I haven't had a decent meal in days. It's all snacks and sandwiches grabbed from the hospital café. It's okay but it's not like a proper meal.'

I grip his hand across the table. 'I'm so sorry about your mum.'

'I know. Me too.' He bites his lip and looks away. 'Have you heard anything from your finance guy?'

'Yes, he sent me an email this morning. All proceeding as requested. With any luck I should have the investment cash back in my account by the end of this week.'

'And the mortgage?'

'He's had two firm offers but he's just waiting for the third which he thinks will be a better rate of interest. I told him it won't be for long as you'll be paying me back, but you know what these money people are like.'

'You emphasised the urgency?'

'Yes, yes. He says it shouldn't be a problem. Early next week the money can be available.'

'And it'll go into your bank account?'

'Yes. Then I can pay you and you can pay for the flat.'

'I'm still nervous. I get the impression that the seller is a bit of a bastard. I think he wants me to default, he wants to take a higher offer, it's a win-win for him, isn't it?'

'We won't let that happen.'

'No, absolutely,' he says. 'I trust you.'

In the night I wake to find Perry crying in his sleep. It's horrible. I try to imagine how I would feel if one of my parents died. It would be horrendous and I, at least, have my siblings to share the burden with. Perry is on his own.

'I'm going to cancel Angie for this weekend,' I tell him in the morning. 'I think we could do with a quiet weekend, just the two of us.'

'Thank you. I appreciate that.'

He leaves mid-morning and I get back to my studio. I do need to get busy especially as I now seem to have two managers nagging at me. One for money, one for love.

He messages me at lunchtime to say he's arrived and that he won't be about for the rest of the afternoon because he's got things to sort out. I tell him I understand.

On Thursday evening he rings me.

'Hey, *min kärlek*,' he says, slightly slurring his words.

'How it's going?' Another crass sounding question from me.

'Well, I'm glad you asked, because you will not fucking believe what's going on here.'

'Perry, have you been drinking?'

'You bet your life I fucking have.'

I'm quite shocked, he really doesn't swear much and hearing him swear twice in a few seconds is frightening.

'Tell me what's happening,' I say.

'Well, where do I start. Tried to arrange the funeral for Mum, lined up an undertaker, they went to collect her body and guess what? The hospital won't release it. Talk about wasting my money…'

I'm almost afraid to ask, 'Why?'

'It appears that she's donated her body to science.'

'Is that even a thing?'

'Yes, it's a fucking thing. And she didn't even have the decency to tell me. Can you believe it? I can't.'

'Can't you challenge it, as her next of kin, I mean?'

'Nope, it's all signed, sealed and delivered. The deal has been done. And get this, I have to pay for the removal of her body from hospital to the medical institute on top of what I already owe the undertaker to not collect her body.'

'Out of her estate,' I muse aloud.

'What's left of it. Ha.' He gives a hollow, bitter laugh. 'I went to the solicitors this afternoon about her will. Again another shocker. She's left everything to a cats' home.'

I'm quite speechless.

'Did you hear me? A cats' home.'

'Yes, yes, I…'

'Yeah, that was my reaction.'

'And you didn't know?'

'Oh, she used to joke about it, years ago. I didn't think she'd actually go and do it. She didn't even like cats, she was always moaning about them crapping on her garden.'

'Oh, Perry, what are you going to do?'

'Nothing, I can't do a thing. I've managed to move some money out of her bank account to cover some of the costs, but as of 10am tomorrow morning I have to be out of here, hand the keys over to the solicitor and it's all out of my hands. Nothing to do with me. Nothing. I'm just grabbing some personal stuff, some photos, bits of jewellery and that's it. Not only am I an orphan now, I don't even get to benefit from her will. It's as though I never existed. As though I wasn't her son.'

Then he ends the call, without even a goodbye.

I hope he doesn't drink too much especially if he has to be up and out of there by ten.

Seventeen

Perry arrives home early afternoon. I hear the front door slam and I rush from my studio to greet him. His face is like thunder. I'm almost afraid to speak.

I stand there waiting for him to say something. He just rips off his jacket and hurls it at the sofa.

I open my mouth then shut it without saying a word.

He glances over at me as though he's only just realised I'm here.

'Sorry I'm a bit later than expected.'

'Oh, you're not.'

'Only once I'd collected all the personal bits, you know photo albums, stuff from my childhood, then handed the keys over, I went straight to my storage unit.'

I nod.

'Yeah, where I've got the few things from my house. Anyway, I've added all that to it. I've got her jewellery too. Left that in the storage unit otherwise I'd be tempted to sell it, which I might regret later. I can't bear to look at the photos, the mementos of old.'

He slumps down on the sofa, then jumps up again and starts pacing the room.

'I cannot believe she did this to me. After all we've been through together.'

He goes to the kitchen tap, runs it, fills a glass and glugs it down in one go. I don't mention the mineral water in the fridge.

'Who sat with her day after day in hospital? Me. That's who. Not some bloody cat. Hours I sat there, holding her hand, soothing her, chatting away. Then just before she died she opened her eyes, saw me and grinned. Then she was gone. And you know what I thought then?' He looks at me though not waiting for an answer he continues, 'I thought how sweet, she's saved all her energy to say goodbye. To leave me with a smile. No, she wasn't saying goodbye she was grinning because she knew what she'd done.'

He slumps back down on the sofa and buries his head in his hands.

'I was a good son to her, I really was. I was her only child. I've spent all my adult years trying to keep her happy and well, trying to please her. Then she does this. The body to science thing is shocking enough but the cats' home. For God's sake. What's was the matter with her?'

'Are you sure you can't challenge it? When did she make this decision? Maybe she was ill, not fit to make such a decision.' I'm trying to help. I think.

He turns and looks at me. 'Don't you think I've explored all that? I have. She made that will ten years ago. Ten fucking years. And she reconfirmed it with her solicitor two years ago. I haven't got a fucking leg to stand on, not one. I've seen my solicitor, not hers obviously, and she said I could spend a fortune contesting it and most likely still wouldn't win not least because the cats' home will fight me vehemently.'

I sit down with him and look down at my hands.

'I don't think I know the woman. I think there was

someone else in there masquerading as my mother.' He takes a deep breath. Then shudders. 'If I didn't have you, Adam, I think I'd just go under. Stop breathing myself.'

I reach over and take his hand. I really don't know what to say. What can I say? What can I do? Nothing is going to make this better. Nothing.

I message Angie and put her off coming for the weekend. When she asks why I tell her that Perry's mum has died. I don't tell her the rest. I can't tell anyone that. It's too awful.

☯☯☯

We have that kind of night's sleep when you're frightened to sleep. I spend the whole night on edge and Perry spends it bouncing around, tossing, turning, cussing in his sleep.

I can't begin to imagine how it must feel to be so betrayed.

He gets up before me and spends a long time in the shower. I'm not tempted to join him. I feel as though I'm dancing on eggshells. I hurriedly use the guest bathroom, quickly dress then head into my studio. I need to get some work done and I need to give Perry some space.

'Hey,' he says from the doorway an hour later.

'Hi.' I turn around and smile, not too brightly; I wouldn't want him to think I don't care.

'You want some breakfast?'

'Er, yeah.' I grab a rag and wipe my hands. 'What would you like?'

'I've made it,' he says, following me along to the kitchen where he's cooking what looks like a Spanish omelette.

'Smells good.' I smile again.

'Ja. It's a fridge omelette.' He laughs to himself. 'I've used up everything in the fridge, you know, the eggs, that tiny bit of cheese, those mushrooms and tomatoes.'

'Oh, great.'

'Yeah, we really need to do some proper food shopping. You never have much here.'

'No, I eat out a lot.'

He eyes me. 'Ja, maybe we should eat in more. Sit down.'

He serves the omelette up, splitting it between us. I have to admit it's good and I'm hungrier than I realised.

'Good?'

'Very good,' I answer.

'Hey, Adam, *min kärlek*, I'm sorry I've been so grumpy. It's not fair on you, any of this.'

'I understand. It's tough on you.'

'Ja. I guess.'

'Anyway, what are fiancés for?'

He gets up, beckons me to do the same and hugs me tight. 'I couldn't get through this without you, Adam. I just couldn't. Have you heard from your finance guy yet?'

'Yes. The money from the investments has come through, came yesterday. In all the… well you know, it went out of my head.'

'That's great. You need to start transferring it to me so I can send it to my solicitor, it's too much to send in one go. There's a limit on online banking transfers, so we've got time to do it in stages. What about the mortgage?'

'Should be through Monday, Tuesday at the latest.'

'Excellent. We can complete before the deadline. When I spoke to my solicitor about… the other business, I asked about the flat, she's completed all the conveyancing, so we're ready to go. I'll be pleased if we can complete before the deadline then I can get that bastard off my back. And it pleases me to know that he'll be losing money because he can't gazump me and keep my deposit.' He smiles then, a proper smile, probably the first one since he's come home.

☯☯☯

Everything goes through and late on Thursday afternoon Perry goes off to collect the keys for the Kensington flat. He's soon back, grinning and waving the keys in front of me.

'That was quick. How does it look now you own it?'

'I haven't been to see it.'

'Oh. Why not?'

'I thought we could go together, tomorrow maybe. Has the online shop arrived yet?'

'Yes, ten minutes after you left so I had to put it away. We have a stuffed fridge. I put your toiletries in the bathroom.'

'Excellent, well done. So, you happy to come to Kensington tomorrow?'

'Yes, I can spare an hour or so.'

'We could pop into Harrods too, if you like.'

'Yeah, okay. But can we go in the morning, I really need to get some work done tomorrow.'

'Of course. Now, let's see what I'm going to cook us for dinner. In the meantime, you can get back to your studio.'

☯☯☯

On Friday morning we visit the flat. It's exactly the same as when we looked at it before except that it seems small.

Perry frowns as he looks around. 'Is it me, or does it seem smaller?'

'I was just thinking that.'

'Ja. I think I've been spoilt by your spacious abode.' He laughs and nudges me. 'So, I think we just let this place as is. No need to furnish it, I think. What do you think?'

'Whatever you want, it's your place.'

He smiles. 'Hey, Adam, what's yours is mine and so on. I'll call a letting agent later and we'll soon have a tenant in here and it can be earning us money. Shall we go to Harrods now?'

We wander around Harrods arm in arm, I'm not really in the mood for shopping so am happy to let Perry take the lead. We soon find ourselves looking at desks. Perry spends a lot of time scrutinising one in particular.

'Are you buying a desk?' I ask, growing bored with the wait and anxious to get back to my studio.

'Maybe. But I think I have one very like this in my storage unit.' He frowns as he tries to remember.

'From your house?'

'No, no. I already had a few items in there, things I originally intended to sell but which took my fancy. I never had room in the house for a desk. Let's go home, unless there's something you'd like to look at?'

'No. No.' I need to get back to work.

It's the evening and after a good homecooked meal by Perry we are slobbing out on the sofa when Perry brings up the desk again.

'I've been thinking, now that I'm living here permanently, officially, I really could do with a workspace.'

'Yes, feel free.'

'I've been using the bedroom and sometimes the

living room but when I attend meetings on Zoom a headboard or a kitchen tile in the background doesn't look very professional.'

'No, I suppose not. I suppose you could squeeze into my studio. We could make an office corner for you.'

He frowns at me, then smiles. 'Not really. You don't want that, do you?'

I shake my head. I don't want to share my studio space with anyone, not even Perry. It's my sanctum, and I need solitude to be creative. I don't even like music playing when I'm working. It's the best space in the whole apartment. Because I bought this place off plan and it was originally intended to be four bedrooms, I was able to stop them building the partitioning for the extra two bedrooms, thus creating my large and light studio.

'I was thinking about the spare bedroom. I could rearrange the furniture a little, make a smart office space with a better wall backdrop. More Zoom meetings mean less travelling too. Which is definitely a bonus when I get to spend more time with you.'

'But Angie sleeps in there.'

'It's a big room. With a bit of rearranging there'll be plenty of room for the bed and my desk. She can still use it when she comes.'

'Yes, I suppose she can. Yes. Go ahead. But don't expect me to hump furniture around.' I laugh, but I'm not joking. I don't do that.

'No problem. Leave it with me.'

Monday comes and I'm hard at work when Perry appears in the doorway.

'It's done,' he says, smiling happily.

'What is?'

'Come and see.' He takes my hand and guides me into the guest bedroom, the one I always think of as Angie's.

'Oh. Wow.'

He's rearranged the entire room, pushed the bed to the far wall as well as fitting in a rather beautiful desk and chair. The desk looks exactly like the one in Harrods. He even has a bookcase lined up where the bed used to be.

'See, plenty of space.'

'Yes.' Although it will be a bit cosy for Angie.

'Look,' he says, sitting down at his desk. 'When I'm on a Zoom call the background is the bookcase. So much better than a headboard, don't you think?'

'I do.' There is no denying that. 'It's great,' I say, because I don't want to upset him by fretting about space for Angie. He's had enough upset lately.

On Tuesday Jasper makes an impromptu visit, although he did suggest on his last visit he would call round to check on my progress. Perry is working away in his office and doesn't come out of the room, which is a relief.

'How are you getting on? How many masterpieces have you completed?' He almost rushes past me on his way to my studio. 'Oh,' he says, turning to me. 'To be honest I expected more.'

'I've been working flat out,' I tell him. It's true, I have when I've been here but there have been too many distractions even then. 'I've finished two out of the three unfinished ones.'

'But you haven't started anything new?'

'No, but…' I wiggle my head around hoping to convey confidence.

'You do know time is ticking away? You do know that Gerard won't accept anything less than eighteen paintings? Ideally he'd like more.'

'There's plenty of time.' I'm beginning to think there isn't.

Jasper raises his eyebrows in question. 'Dear boy, if you're struggling do say and we can postpone. As I said before Pitney-Goddard's agent is champing at the bit for the gallery space and is almost crawling backwards up Gerard's bum to try to secure it. So you do have the option to postpone.'

'I don't want to postpone, least of all for him.'

'Okay. I need to go now, but I'll be back next week and I do expect to see significant progress.' He turns and flounces out of my studio and heads for the door. I follow behind glad to be rid of him. 'I'm surprised at you, Adam, it's so unlike you. Is it *him*? Is he affecting your concentration?' He yanks the door open and marches out.

I stand leaning against the doorframe as he calls the lift then disappears into it, breathing a sigh of relief when he's gone.

'That was Jasper?' Perry asks.

'Woah,' I yell, jumping. 'I didn't know you were there.

'I could hear him speaking to you and I have to say I don't like it one little bit. How dare he speak to you like that. You're his client. Without you he'd be nothing. We'll compose an email together later and let him know who's boss. And we can start with ending his impromptu visits.'

'Oh. Right. Yeah.'

'I won't have you spoken to like that, *min kärlek*. I just won't allow it.'

Eighteen

Jasper doesn't even reply to the email we send. Not even an acknowledgment. Perhaps it was a bit harsh. Perry drafted it and allowed me to soften it a little, but maybe not enough. I'm beginning to worry that he didn't get it and will turn up unannounced again.

I put Angie off visiting again because Perry has a couple of important Zoom meetings over the coming weekend. When I ring her to explain, she just sighs. On the plus side Perry and I will be visiting next month for my mum's birthday, so they'll all get to meet him.

It's Tuesday and there's still no response from Jasper. I'm now very worried that he'll turn up like he has the last two Tuesdays. Maybe I should pre-empt his arrival by ringing him. Perry's working from home today and I don't want a repeat of last week. I don't know how Perry will react if he thinks Jasper is being rude to me, but I don't think it will be pleasantly.

I pick up my phone and begin to scroll for Jasper's number when a message pops up from him. He must have been feeling my angst.

Jasper: *Progress update please. And send photos of any new works.*

Me: *Hi Jasper. Nice to hear from you. Will send soon. Hope you are well. A xx*

Am I pushing my luck with that message? Probably, because he doesn't reply.

I go into the studio and take a photograph of the third original unfinished piece which I have finally finished. I've also started a new painting. I take a photo of that too. I don't take a photo of what I've really been working on because it's not for exhibition and it's certainly not for sale.

I send the photos and grit my teeth as I wait for Jasper to respond. I can see that he's seen the message.

After an hour I have to message him again.

Me: *Did you get my photos?*

Jasper: *Yes, but only two. Waiting for the rest.*

Oh damn it, there are no more.

Me: *That's it at the moment.*

Jasper: *Tick tock, last chance. Send me proper progress by Monday otherwise we'll have to postpone.*

Then he goes offline. From his tone it's obvious he's annoyed, and probably offended by my email. I shouldn't have sent it; I should have rung him up. Now I feel I can't.

I need to knuckle down and work, work, work. I'm just getting into it when Perry appears in the studio doorway, rubbing his neck.

'Hey, I'm going a bit stir crazy here, fancy going out for lunch? My treat of course.' He grins at me. His grin is so damned disarming.

I put down my paintbrush. 'Go on then, but I can't be long.'

☯☯☯

We've been away over two hours and we've had wine. I

don't feel very productive now but I need to force myself back into my studio. Perry says he's had a very productive morning and needs to chill this afternoon. He's brought out a game player, a brand-new PlayStation, it's still in the box when he brings it into the living room. I leave him to it but once in the studio I can hear the noise it makes, guns blazing, cars racing.

I'm rather surprised at Perry, he's pushing forty and this doesn't seem like his vibe at all. It seems at complete odds to his passion for vintage Swedish furniture.

The following weekend I put my sister off visiting again because I need to get cracking with my work. I don't like working weekends, but I have no choice.

Despite my hardest efforts I only produce one more finished piece, plus the one I'd already started earlier.

I message my progress to Jasper.

He replies immediately. It isn't good.

Jasper: *Saddened to ask if that is it? Also, cannot believe I am saying this to you and maybe it's the way the paintings have photographed lately but the quality doesn't look up to your usual standard. Tell me they look better in real life.*

I can't. He's right. I don't perform well under constant pressure.

Me: *I think you'd better postpone. I'm not feeling it at the moment. Apologies.*

Jasper: *Sorry to hear that. Are you ill?*

Me: *I'm fine. You take care of yourself.*

I hope he doesn't reply. I don't want to discuss it further. However, two days later he does.

Jasper: *Postponed as per your instruction. Gerard says he won't reschedule until you have enough pieces to show. So pressure is completely off. Hope that helps your creativity.*

I admit I do feel less stressed now. I tell Perry about the situation, the first time I've mentioned Jasper's name since the email went.

'Maybe you should look for another agent,' Perry says, his tone dismissive. 'I do wonder if he has been representing you properly, getting the right amount of cash for your works, taking the right commission. We should shop around for someone else.'

'But I've been with Jasper for… well, always.'

'Then maybe it's time to shake things up, *min kärlek*. Ja?'

'I don't know.'

'I think there must be dozens of agents desperate to snap up the great Adam Hames RA. Don't you worry. Hey, maybe I'll represent you myself.'

'But you don't know anything about the art world. You admitted as much.'

'Hey, it's selling. I know about selling. Ja? I know about making money.' He wraps his arms around me in a great bear hug and I feel comforted, a little.

'I'm not going to ditch Jasper just yet,' I say, untangling myself from Perry's hug.

'No. Of course not.' He laughs, then wanders off to play his games again. He seems to be unwinding with his games a lot of late.

With the pressure off I spend more time in my studio. Not that I am as productive as I would like or expect to be. I seem to spend an awful lot of time staring across the river or tinkering with my little vanity project.

I put Angie off again and actually tell her it might be indefinite. Much as Perry wants to meet her, he says he does do quite a bit of business at weekends and that means privacy for his Zoom calls, that or he'll have to go back to flying here, there and everywhere.

I'm also concerned about money. Very. I'm running low on funds just to pay the household bills, and of course, the mortgage I now have. I've never paid a massive amount of attention to my finances, that's why I have an accountant and a financial advisor, but my bank has been pinging me about funds running low, something I've never experienced before. Perry is now buying all the food but even I've noticed an increase in the electric bill since he moved in, which I suppose was inevitable. I've never given such things a second thought in the past; perhaps this is how it feels for Angie. It's my own fault; to enable Perry to buy the Kensington flat I've cleaned myself out. And I've increased my outgoings.

Is this what's affecting my creativity?

☯☯☯

We're approaching the weekend at my parents' place for my mum's birthday. I'm excited that everyone will finally get to meet Perry. This weekend is a big deal for my mum as she's turning seventy. She's having a big party. It's the perfect opportunity for my fiancé to see what he's marrying into. Not that we've discussed the wedding lately; Perry says he wants our finances straight before we organise anything. And that means his house sale going through smoothly.

'What's the situation with your house sale?' I ask him one morning.

He shrugs. 'Slow,' he says. 'Those people are dragging their heels. I just hope it means they will go through with it. Not like the last lot who pushed and pushed then backed out at the last minute.'

'Yeah,' I say, sounding pensive.

'Everything okay, *min kärlek?*'

I don't know whether to say anything, then chide myself. I must say something. 'Funds are a bit tight,' I say, trying not to grit my teeth.

'Really? How tight?'

'Well, I used to get income from my investments. I don't anymore. I pretty much cleaned out my accounts to help you and I now have a mortgage to pay.' I feel embarrassed even saying this stuff. 'And the bills have increased.'

'Not the food bill.' He raises his eyebrows. 'Or the eating out bill, ja?'

'True. But I don't have much in the way of income now and with my show at Gerard's postponed indefinitely…'

'Ja, I see. Why didn't you say something before, *min kärlek?*' He wraps me in his bear hug. 'You can be silly at times. I'll send some cash to your account. Will two thousand do for now?'

I do quick calculation, then grimace.

'Three thousand?'

I nod and smile.

'Good, I'll send it today to your account. Don't worry, *min kärlek*. Just ask if you need more.'

'I may need more.'

'Let me know when.' He grins at me and I worry that I'll be asking for more fairly soon.

I steel myself. 'Do you think you could make a regular payment?'

He frowns at me. 'Ja. Okay. How much would you need?'

'Until you can pay me back I need enough to cover the mortgage and the bills, so the same again, every month.' And even that will be just about enough.

He looks me up and down, appraising, considering. 'You're right. I should cover the mortgage. We can deduct it from the final payment. And yes, my darling, I should be paying to live here. It's very remiss of me. I've been so wound up in my business, and my mother's situation, I haven't been thinking straight. I'll make a regular payment. We can't have you worrying about finances when you're supposed to be creative.' He kisses me on the head and I feel an immense weight lift from my shoulders. 'And I'm going to give you shares in the company, that should provide a nice income until your paintings start to sell again.'

'Wow, thank you. I wasn't expecting that.'

'It'll take a little while to organise, but then you'll start getting the dividends. I'll get my legal guy on it.'

☯☯☯

Tonight we're travelling down to my parents' home. I'm so damn excited. I've not mentioned it much to Perry because I don't want him to be nervous. Weeks ago, when I suggested the idea, he expressed concern that I come from such a large family and he had no one. But I told him that now he's marrying me my family will become his. We're driving because it's easier and I've pulled out my large suitcase. I think Perry and I should share.

'What's that?' he says, coming out of the bathroom, still drying his hair with a towel. It's grown even longer now than when I first met him.

'Your hair is coming in even fairer than the rest,' I say, ribbing him.

'You don't think it's going grey, do you?' He rushes over to the mirror, pulling his hair away from his face to examine the roots. 'Or white? Argh.'

'No. Anyway, would it make any difference? Would anyone be able to tell?'

'Suppose not.' He grins at his reflection then turns back to me. 'So, what's that?'

'I thought we'd take one large suitcase instead of two smaller ones.'

He frowns.

'We haven't got to pull them anywhere, no airports or train stations.'

He looks at me blankly for a moment too long then realisation dawns.

'It's this weekend, your parents?'

'Yes. I have been talking about it for weeks.'

He puffs out a long breath and slumps onto the bed.

'It'll be great. My family will love you as much as I do. And you and Angie will really hit it off.'

'It's not that,' he says. 'Oh Adam, I've really fucked up.'

'What do you mean?'

He sighs again, slumps lower on the bed, hangs his head. 'There is this guy in Akersberga, I've been speaking to him on Zoom for weeks. He has some chairs, mid-century, wishbone chairs by Hans Wegner. They're originals, not copies. He has ten. They're going to cost me a fortune but I have a buyer in America who is desperate for them. I've been setting this deal up for weeks.' He puts his hands in his head.

'Can't you go on Monday, or some other time?'

'I would, you know I would. But I can't because the American buyer must have them next week. That's why I have to go to Akersberga myself, to arrange the shipping.' He looks up at me, tears in his eyes. 'I've so fucked up.'

I'm devastated.

'Can't you get someone else to ship them.'

He shakes his head. 'I can't. The deal isn't sealed. The

owner wants to meet me in person, wants to see the whites of my eyes.' He rolls his eyes as he says this. 'He wants to see the colour of my money too.'

'He doesn't trust you?'

'It's not me specifically. He's been crossed in the past, so he's super cautious. It's tomorrow or no time. He's being very demanding. But this deal is going to make so much money for the business, keep the shareholders happy.' He nudges me.

I slump down onto the bed next to him.

'Maybe I could let it slide. Meeting your family is more important. I need to keep my future in-laws sweet.'

I'm too shellshocked to reply.

'Just say the word and I'll cancel.'

'No, no. Go ahead. We can visit my family another time, might be better when it's a bit less frenzied there. Just the two of us.'

'*Min kärlek*, if you're sure.'

'Yes, you go ahead. They'll understand.'

☯☯☯

It's Friday evening and I've just arrived at my parents. I pull my, now small, bag out of the boot and head for the front door. The plan is that tonight is a family dinner, which would have been the perfect time for them to meet Perry; tomorrow is the big party.

The door flies open and Angie stands grinning before me. She flings her arms around my neck and hugs me so tight, reaching up and letting her feet dangle in the air, that my neck aches.

'So long,' she screeches. Finally letting go, she peers beyond me. 'Where is he then? Where are you hiding him?'

‘He can’t make it.’

‘Whatttt?’

‘I know, business, last minute, important.’ I sound as though I’m speaking in code.

‘Oh but I was so looking forward to meeting him.’

‘I know. He was looking forward to meeting everyone too, especially you.’

‘I’ll have to come up and sort him out,’ she says, with a grin before leading me inside. ‘Mum and Dad are upstairs getting ready. You’re in the posh guest room.’

‘And where are you sleeping tonight?’

‘Strictly speaking I should go home, but if I don’t make it I’m in your old room.’

That makes me smile. My old room is tiny, tucked under the eaves and is especially noisy when it rains. I have fond memories of that room, it’s where I planned my early paintings, often sketching them out on the tiny desk tucked into the corner. ‘You’ll be cosy in there,’ I say.

‘I know. You’re only getting the posh room because you were bringing him. I think you should have your old room now, you fraud.’ She grins at me.

‘No, if you drink too much you can get a taxi home.’

‘Spoilsport.’

It’s lovely to see my parents again, I haven’t seen them since Christmas. I never did make it down for Mother’s Day, though I did send a very expensive bouquet. My mum doesn’t mind, my dad has other opinions.

They’ve booked an entire restaurant, owned by one of their friends, for a family only dinner. There are so many of us, children included, that we easily fill the place and their friend’s takings are probably higher that they usually would be on a Friday night. Everyone asks where Perry is. I have to repeat his business meeting plans so many times I feel like just sending everyone a group message. But, eventually, as the night wears on they forget about him.

There are the inevitable jokes and ribbing about me being famous, rich and spoilt by my own success. I remind them all that my success is due to my hard work and talent and that they've all benefited from it many times when they've fancied a weekend in London. Not that many of them come now, not so much since they all had children. Except Angie, of course. It's all good-natured fun and in return I rib my brothers about being boring solicitors.

The party on Saturday night is a big, busy affair. To drown my sorrows I drink too much. Angie, having spent Friday night in my childhood bedroom decides enough is enough and gets a taxi back to her own flat. When I wake up on Sunday morning I feel awful, I had far too much to drink last night and unlike Friday night, not enough food to soak it up.

I check my phone to see if Perry has replied to the many messages I have sent him over the weekend, but he hasn't. I suppose he's not getting them, connection problems maybe. Still he'll be home late tonight, and I'll be home before him; maybe I'll cook something nice. Me cooking, that will make a change. He'll be glad of a home cooked meal after his flight.

I'm sitting eating a leisurely breakfast with Mum and Dad when my phone pings. Ah, finally Perry has connectivity. But it's not Perry, it's Jasper. And he's not happy.

Jasper: *Think your email to me was the lowest of the low. How dare you after all these years? You won't be having any kind of show in Gerard's gallery, or any other London galleries if I have anything to do with it.*

I'm confused. Has he only just received the email I sent him weeks ago? No, that can't be right. That just asked him not to come round and he's complied with that.

Me: *What you do you mean? What email?*

Jasper replies with a series of rolling-eye emojis.

I scroll through my phone and check my emails, finding the sent ones. There's nothing from me to him so I message him to that affect.

He replies with a screenshot of the email. It certainly looks as though it's from me.

Apparently, I've sacked him.

Nineteen

I've rung Jasper six times now. Three before I left my parents and three since I got back. I've left one very long, grovelling voicemail explaining that I don't know what's going on and that I didn't send that email.

I'm sure there's been some weird misunderstanding with this email business and Jasper. I never sent that email. I've definitely been hacked, the sooner he believes that, the better.

He hasn't replied.

I've distracted myself by cooking. I've made a lasagne, one of the few things I can cook, other than breakfast which is my speciality. Angie and I once spent an afternoon at a pseudo-Italian cookery class, by the end we could both make lasagne. It just needs about forty minutes in the oven later. I'm looking forward to Perry's arrival. He still hasn't messaged or rung me but he's probably in the air now, on route back to London, or his phone battery has died again. I refuse to imagine him in another car accident. It couldn't happen twice.

Perry never gave me a time he'd be home but I've checked the planes from Stockholm, which is where he has to fly from, and the last one today got in about twenty minutes ago. So I'm putting the lasagne in the oven now.

Perry should have been home an hour ago, even accounting for traffic which really shouldn't be bad at this time on a Sunday night. I've messaged him repeatedly, and rung and rung. Nothing. The lasagne is cooling on top of the oven. We can always microwave it when he gets in, assuming he's still hungry. I was hungry but my appetite has faded away. I hope Perry is all right. I hope nothing has happened to him.

It's midnight now. No sign of Perry. Did he definitely say he was coming home tonight? I'm starting to doubt myself. Was it tonight or tomorrow night? No, Sunday, I'm sure, I think.

Daylight wakes me. I'm on the sofa, cold and uncomfortable. The TV is still on; I used it as a distraction last night. I check my phone for news from Perry, there is none. I ring him, his phone rings out. I send yet another message. I must have the day wrong; it must be today he's coming home.

I shower and dress and feel like shit. I force myself to eat some cereal. At least I had the foresight to put the lasagne in the fridge last night, we can have it tonight when he comes home. I check my phone, nothing. Neither from Perry nor Jasper.

Jasper is obviously sulking, and Perry's phone must have a flat battery. I think we need to sort him out a new phone, a one with better battery life. Maybe I need to check when he goes away that he always has his power bank. In a minute he'll come bursting in here full of annoyance because his phone has died.

After breakfast I make an effort and head to my studio; I might as well use my time productively.

Something's amiss in the studio. I don't know what. I scurry round and check that my special project has not been disturbed. It's a small canvas which I've kept covered and hidden behind my larger pieces. I can't find it; I can't find it. But it must be here somewhere. It'll turn up. I know it will. I take a deep breath, calm myself. I need to stop catastrophising. The painting is here. Perry is safe.

I go to my easel, pull on my paint-spattered jacket and pick up my brush. That's when I notice it. I wonder how I could have missed it. There's another painting missing. It's the one that Jasper admired, raved over in fact. Has he been round and taken it? Has he had it parcelled up and couriered away? Has he taken my special project too? If so, where to?

Then it dawns on me, he has no key to my apartment any longer. He cannot get in. Which means that he must have arrived, or sent his couriers, when Perry was still here. I'm surprised that Perry allowed him to take a painting without letting me know. Really surprised.

I try to work but constantly check my phone for word from Perry. Or Jasper. I try both again. Leave a long message on Perry's phone but also knowing that if the battery is flat, he won't hear it anyway. I don't leave a message for Jasper, I said everything I could in my last message. I hope he comes to his senses and believes I've been hacked.

I'm confused about the missing painting. Maybe Gerard's decided to show that one after all. I smile to myself. How funny that would be if my painting was the centrepiece to Pitney-Goddard's show. Would Gerard do that?

☯☯☯

I've been dozing on the sofa and now it's getting dark. There's no sign of Perry. I've left the lasagne in the fridge. I'm very worried. I ring him again. This time the call goes straight to that message, "the number you have dialled has not been recognised." I think he's either lost his phone or had it stolen. Now he's reported it and it's been cut off. Definitely time to get him a new phone. Maybe that can be my treat, an engagement present since he didn't want a ring. I admire my own ring in the half light, then get up to check the time.

There's still no sign of him. I check the plane arrivals. He should have been home by now. Where the hell is he? Is he dead somewhere? I feel my heart beat rapidly at the thought. I cannot bear to lose him. Not now I've finally found him. The one. My one.

Why hasn't he rung me, let me know what's going on? Ah, if he's lost his phone he won't know the number. Who memorises phone numbers now? My parents still have an address book they keep phone numbers in. No one my age does that.

Where is he?

It's late, he should be here. Maybe he's so tired he's asleep in his car. Maybe he's down in the car park snoring away, his head slumped over the wheel. I grab my keys and go down to check.

His car isn't there? It wasn't there when I came back so he definitely has it. What if he's been in an accident?

I don't know what to do. I don't know who to call.

Back up in my flat I take a deep breath and pull myself together. I need to find him. I make a list.

Hospitals

Police, but not 999 it should be... what 911? No, that's the US. I google it. It's 101.

I ring 101. The operator isn't scathing but she isn't sympathetic either. She suggests I ring around his friends to track him down. I hang up feeling dejected.

I check the traffic news for information on fatal accidents.

I ring three hospitals; the operators take my details and say they'll ring back if they find anything. Which means they won't ring back.

Then it dawns on me, he may have changed his plans. The logical place to look would be in his office, on his desk.

Why didn't I think of that before?

In his office there is no desk. No chair. No bookcase. The bed is back in its original position. It's as if he's never been here.

I run to our bedroom; fling open his wardrobe door. Nothing. Just a few empty hangers, old ones, mine not his. I check the bedside drawer. Nothing. I check the bathroom, looking for his toiletries. Nothing. I rush around the apartment looking for any sign of him, anything. No evidence of the irritating games console. There is nothing. How could I have been so blind? How could I have missed this?

I twiddle the engagement ring on my finger. This is real. Isn't it?

Am I going mad?

I slump onto the sofa and finally slide into a sleep of exhaustion. Deep but fretful.

What the hell is going on?

☯☯☯

Dawn is breaking when I awake and I force myself through the motions, make coffee, take it out onto the terrace to drink. It's chilly, the city is waking, the river is moving. Perry is still missing.

Where the hell is Perry?

I find my phone, now my battery is flat. I hunt for my charger – I'm always losing my charger, so often that Perry has bought me a second one – but I find it and plug my phone in. Check for messages. Nothing from Jasper, nothing from Perry.

Ring round his friends the police said. Who are his friends? I've not met any of his friends. None of my friends or family have met Perry.

No one has met Perry.

Yes, Martin has met Perry on the day we spoke about security. No, it wasn't Martin, it was one of the many other ones.

I race down to Martin. He has a woman at his desk. He's smiling and helpful. Go away, go away. Finally she goes.

'Martin, have you seen Perry lately?'

'Perry, sir?'

'My partner. My fiancé. He lives with me. You must have seen him.'

'Not that I recall, sir.' He moves a pen on his desk as I lean over the top looking down, as though the answer lies there. 'Is there anything else I can help you with?'

I ask him, who was working on that day?

'Which day would that be, sir?'

'The day we came down to change the arrangements. You weren't here. It was a week day. I think it was a week day.' When was it? 'When were you not here? Whoever it was ordered another car barrier fob for me, for Perry. Who was it?'

Martin stares at me as though I've asked how deep are all the oceans, how high is the sky. As though I am mad.

'Well, sir, I've had a few days off here and there. I could go through the rotas later and check. Then I can get back to you.'

'Can't you do it now?'

'Not really, sir.' He glances beyond me; a courier is waiting with a parcel. It reminds me.

'Did a courier come over the weekend to collect some paintings from my place?'

'Sir,' he says, his smile so professional. 'Why don't you take a seat while I deal with this gentleman.' He waves his hand at a chair while nodding at the courier.

I flop down.

Dealing with the parcel takes ages. The package has to be signed for, then it has to be signed in, then it has to be placed in a locked cupboard until the recipient comes home. The wait is driving me mad. I jump up.

'Well?' I ask, peering over Martin's desk again.

He flicks through his book, the one he's just used to sign in the package.

'No sir, no sign of any couriers visiting you over the weekend.'

'Are you sure?'

'Absolutely.'

'What about furniture removal?' I sound mad even to me.

'Sir?'

'A desk, a chair, a bookcase?'

'No record sir. Nothing in or out all weekend.'

I stand there gaping like a fish, Martin looks at me sadly, then throws me a crumb.

'Of course sir, someone could have taken it straight to the car park. I can't see the far lift from here.'

'Yes, that could be it, couldn't it?'

He smiles. 'And sir, I will get back to you with dates when I haven't been here. Have you any idea when it was so I can narrow my search down a little.'

'A few months,' I say, turning and wandering back to the lift.

Back in my apartment I check my phone for messages. Of course there are none.

Am I mad?

Have I made up this man?

No one has met him. None of my friends. Not my family. Not even Jasper.

What the hell is wrong with me?

I can't have made all that up. Him, us.

I flick through my phone, bring up the photo gallery, look for Stockholm, Amsterdam, Edinburgh, the sly photos I've taken of Perry.

Nothing. Not one.

The entry phone rings and I leap up.

It's Martin.

'Sir, I've checked the dates I haven't been here and there are only two in the last few months. The same person covered for me on both occasions.'

'Excellent. Who is he? When's he here again? I need to talk to him.'

'He was an agency worker, sir.'

'Then ring the agency, Martin.'

'I have, sir, I have. He no longer works for them and they can't give me his details due to data protection, but they will pass on my details to him so he can contact me. That's all we can do at the moment, sir.'

'Great. Thanks.' I put the phone down.

In the kitchen I rummage through the cupboards until I find it, an old bottle of brandy. I don't even like the stuff, but the champagne in the fridge seems wholly inappropriate. I take the brandy out onto the terrace, slump into a chair and decide to drink myself into oblivion.

Twenty

I wake freezing cold. I've fallen asleep on the terrace sofa. The putrid smell of vomit lingers in my nostrils. My own vomit. I could have choked on it.

I drop the empty brandy bottle in the bin. I won't be doing that again. It has solved nothing and now I feel horrendous. I run the cold tap in the kitchen, fill a glass and knock it back, then another. Perry does this. Then I make coffee and take it over to the sofa where I doze again, waking up to cold coffee and cold morning light. I've left the terrace doors wide open and I can't even be bothered to get up and close them.

I don't know what to do. I flick the TV on.

On breakfast TV they're talking about the soaring price of houses, especially in the capital.

Of course, of course, that's where he's gone. Kensington. His new place. I grab my keys.

The traffic is slow, it's rush hour and I really didn't think this through. But it's the time I'm most likely to find him, isn't it? Having breakfast, getting ready for a day of work. I hope he's not away on business.

I abandon the car in a parking bay. I won't be long. When `I press the buzzer for his flat, no one replies. Damn it. I press again and again. No response. I could press others. That's what I'll do, say it's a delivery. Just then someone comes out and I nip in before the door closes behind them.

There's no lift to the top floor. It's something that would have put me off buying it, but probably only because I think of having paintings lugged up and down the stairs, not very practical.

Finally I'm outside his door. It's probably pointless because he never answered the buzzer. I knock.

The door is opened quickly by a woman, smart and obviously ready for work. Who the hell is she? She looks me up and down and doesn't manage to suppress a look of horror.

'Yes?'

'Is Perry in?'

'Who?'

'Ah, I see. Are you the tenant?'

She looks me up and down again. 'I think you have the wrong flat.' She moves to shut the door but I'm too quick for her and shove my foot in the way. She's quick too, pushes her own foot against the inside of the door so I can't get in.

'No, I haven't. This is definitely the one. My friend Perry owns this flat. I thought he might be here. You're his tenant. Have you seen him at all? Has he been round?'

'I don't know any Perry. *I'm* the owner. Get your foot out of the way before I ring the police.' She waves her phone at me.

Reluctantly I move my foot. 'If you see him…'

She slams the door in my face.

I check the landing; I check the floor number. I'm definitely in the right place, the right flat. I'm confused. Has he sold the flat on? Without telling me?

He's probably gone back to his house; the sale hasn't

gone through yet. Of course that's where he is. I run down the stairs, almost fall. Get into my car, notice the parking ticket stuck on the windscreen only once I'm inside. I reach out, rip it off and hurl it away.

It takes forever to get to his house. This is not a part of London I'm over familiar with. I've only been here a few times. But I screech up outside the house and watch for signs of life. What am I expecting?

A deep breath and I get out. Knock on the door. Wait and wait. I knock again. He's not here.

I turn to walk away when the door is suddenly opened by a man. He smiles at me, waiting for me to speak.

'Is Perry here?'

'Who?'

'The owner.'

The man frowns at me then shakes his head. 'No.'

'Who are you?'

'Who are you?' he counters.

'I'm Perry's… it doesn't matter. Are you the new owner?'

'Yes.' He eyes me suspiciously.

'Sorry to disturb you. I'm looking for the old owner. I thought he might be here. I didn't realise it was done.'

The man shakes his head slowly. 'It was an old woman who owned this house but she died almost a year ago. We bought it from her family. It was a probate sale.'

'No, that can't be right.'

'It is.'

'How long have you lived here?'

'Weeks,' he says. 'Sorry, but I'm busy.' With that, he shuts the door.

I get in the car and take a slow drive home. I don't really care how long it takes me. Have I imagined Perry? Conjured him up out of nowhere? Am I going quietly insane?

When I get home I ring Jasper. He doesn't answer so I leave a long message telling him Perry is missing and asking him to ring me.

Then I fall asleep on the sofa again, no wonder given how little decent sleep I've had.

☯☯☯

The shrill tones of the entry phone wake me with a start and I stagger over to answer it.

It's Martin, maybe he's tracked down the agency worker, the one who can verify Perry's existence.

'I have a visitor for you?'

'Is it Perry?'

'It's Jasper,' a voice shouts in the background.

'Yeah, okay.'

I leave the front door open then wander back to the sofa, slump down.

'Adam,' Jaspers says, coming in and closing the door. 'What's been going on?'

'Perry has disappeared.' I feel myself start to crumble. I'm going to cry. I don't want to cry.

Jasper doesn't say anything, just glances around the room, scrutinises me, walks over to the terrace doors and closes them as I get up and follow him.

'You have heard of Perry?' I gulp in air.

'Of course. Your fiancé.'

I look at the ring on my finger. I haven't imagined that. It's very real.

'You've seen Perry, haven't you, Jasper?'

'No,' he says.

'But you've been here when he's been here. In another room, but you knew he was here?'

'I think so. Yes. I'm sure he was here. What's this about, Adam?'

'He's gone. It's like he's never been here. I can find no trace of him. I've been to his house and his apartment and…' I shake my head, then slip down the bifold doors and slide to the floor.

'When was your cleaner last in?'

'Oh, Perry gave her a few weeks off.'

'Indeed. She'll be earning her money when she comes back.' He bends over and picks up a shoe and sock. 'You look like shit. Are you all right?'

'Clearly not.' I haul myself up.

Jasper turns full circle looking around the room.

'Do you think he's real? Do you think I imagined him? Have you ever seen any evidence of him here?'

'I've hardly been here lately. When did you last eat?' He opens the fridge. He pulls a bottle of milk from the door, lifts the lid, sniffs the milk, then pours the contents into the sink. 'Go and have a shower and a shave and whatever else you need to do. Then we're going for lunch. And we can discuss this rationally. Get to the bottom of it. You'll feel a lot better once you're clean and fed.' He takes my shoulders, guides me towards my bedroom, goes into the bathroom and turns on the shower. I half expect him to undress me. 'I'll be in the living room when you're ready.'

☯☯☯

We take a slow walk to Bib and Tucker, the restaurant where I first met Perry. He tells me that he takes all his best clients there. I think he says this to calm me down. It's familiar, it's easy. He orders for both of us and I don't argue. But there's no wine on the table, just sparkling water.

'Tell me from the beginning,' he says, a soft smile on his face.

'First of all, I didn't sack you, Jasper. I just want you to know that.'

'I know. You were hacked.'

'I was. I can't find any evidence of me sending that email.'

He leans over and presses my hand. 'Don't worry about that. Tell me about Perry.'

So I tell him everything. Our meeting, the trips to Stockholm and Amsterdam, our engagement, Perry's house sale falling through. Me lending him the money to buy the Kensington flat. Everything, including how his mother left her money to a cat's home and her body to medical science. He says nothing while I blurt it all out. He doesn't look shocked or judgemental. He's my good friend Jasper.

He excuses himself to go to the loo and when he comes back I ask him, 'Do you believe me?'

'Of course I do, but we need to find evidence. Are you sure nobody ever met him?'

'Yes. No, wait. Angie saw him once on a video call. He was in the background but he called over a hello. She asked if his hair was really that blond. I'd forgotten that. I'll ring her now.' I pull my phone out and call her. It goes to voicemail so I leave a message telling her to call me back urgently. 'She'll be at work,' I tell him. 'Probably in a meeting or something.'

'There, when she rings back we can establish that you're not mad. Other evidence…' he says, frowning slightly.

I shrug.

'Money. You know what they say in films: Follow the

money.' He picks up my phone from the table and hands it to me. 'Banking app?'

'Yes.'

'Log in. Let's see where the money's gone.'

I manage to log in but after that it's a struggle. After watching me, Jasper holds out his hand. 'May I?' I pass the phone over and wait. Sweat is forming on my brow, cold sweat. Supposing I have imagined everything. What does that make me?

Reflected in Jasper's glasses, the numbers on my phone flash by. Finally he looks up, he half smiles.

'Ah, a lot of transactions. Big amounts. Then nothing for a while. There is one payment that has come in recently, for three thousand pounds.'

I nod vigorously. 'Yes, Perry agreed to pay me monthly until he could pay me back in full.'

Looking over the rims of his glasses Jasper continues, 'There's evidence of this mortgage you mentioned coming in from another bank. There's an entry from some financial services company paying in a lot to you.'

'Yes, that's my advisor, he does all my investments. The other one is the mortgage I got on my flat to help Perry out. He's supposed to be paying it all back. You're brilliant, Jasper. I don't know why I didn't think of this. Follow the money. Ha. You're brilliant.' I used to be the brilliant one.

'It's all gone out to one account.'

'Yes, Perry's. So I'm not mad.'

'No. I don't think so. Not that kind of mad, anyway…'

'No, not mad at all, what do you mean?'

Jasper doesn't speak. He just gives me a pitying look.

'What?'

''Well…'

Then it dawns on me. I know what Jasper is thinking because I'm now thinking it too. 'Have I… have I been… scammed?'

'Darling boy, I think you might have been.'

Right then is when the waiter appears and puts the food down in front of us. It's excellent timing because if I had already eaten it I would now be throwing it back up. As it is, I just sit and stare and grip my stomach as I lean over. Jasper motions for the waiter to take our plates away.

'What am I going to do? What am I going to do?' Cold sweat is forming on my forehead.

'Police. You could try the bank. I suspect they'll quote that data protection nonsense and won't help. But the police will be able to get past all that.'

I grab a napkin and wipe my face.

'My dear boy, what are we going to do with you? At least you have your art. Thank God for that.'

'Did you take a painting? That one you admired?'

He shakes his head. 'No.'

'I think he's stolen that painting too. And another,' I add, thinking of my special project. Part of his plan to remove any evidence. I grab my water glass and take a drink.

'Are you feeling any better now? Are you able to eat? You really should eat. They're keeping our food warm.' He waves over at the waiter.

'Err, yes, I'm going to need my strength to track that bastard down.'

'Fighting spirit. That's what we want to see.'

'But Jasper, it was so good. He was so good. He brought out the best in me. Do you think there's been some mistake?'

'When I was looking at your phone I looked at your

photo gallery too. There are big gaps. BIG gaps. He's been through and deleted all evidence of you and him. He's left very little trace. He wanted you to think you were mad. Of course he couldn't delete the financial evidence…'

Deep down I know he's right. I know I've been taken for fool. But deep inside I know I loved Perry. I really believe he loved me, maybe just a little. I force a smile. 'He almost succeeded.' I take a mouth full of food. I can't taste anything but my body craves the nourishment. 'Will you come to the police with me?'

'Absolutely.'

'Should we ring them first? Make an appointment?'

'Does it work like that? I've no idea.' Jasper smiles at me. 'However it works we'll get through it. You have me, you have Angie, you have your family. We'll get you through this.'

I glance at my phone wondering when Angie will ring back. Should I call her again? Maybe I'll wait. I take another mouthful of food, stare absently out of the window as I chew the meat which seems a little tough but I won't complain; it's probably my fault anyway as they had to keep it warm. I feel wretched. I feel stupid. But I will get through this. I will.

'How could I have been so naïve?'

'He's quite the professional, I would say. You're probably not the first.'

'His mother, I wonder if she was really his mother?'

'We have to make sure you're the last. And we have to get your money back, or at least some of it.'

'Yes, yes, we do. Thank you for helping me. Thank you.' I stare out of the window again. 'Do you think we'll get my money…. It's him.' I jump up, Perry is wandering past on the other side of the road seemingly without a care in the world. He's wearing a pale blue hat to hide his distinctive hair and it looks as though he hasn't shaved for days but I'd recognise that lovely face anywhere.

'Adam what…?' Jasper calls, as I run out after Perry.

He's heading for the Tube. I can see him turning down the Underground steps. If I call out his name will he hear me?

'Perry. Perry,' I yell. A woman near me flinches but Perry doesn't stop.

Down the steps he flies. Down the steps I follow. His hat is helping, it's so distinctive.

'Perry,' I call again.

This time he turns, glances back, but he doesn't stop and I don't know if he sees me.

I reach the turnstile. I have no ticket, no Oyster card. I can see him disappearing into a tunnel.

I leap the barrier. I run after him. I don't call his name; I just keep that blue hat in sight.

We reach the platform. He's ahead of me and I think I can reach him. It's so crowded. So many people just milling around waiting. Perry nudges up the platform. A gush of wind wafts through the tunnel. I barge my way through. Perry is stationery. I reach out my hand to grab his shoulder. He turns. It's him. It's him. He looks alarmed. Then the look changes to amusement. He shrugs off my hand. Smiles at me. Winks.

His lovely face is the last thing I see.

Twenty-one

ANGIE

Gray and I spent the weekend tiptoeing around each other. Me to avoid him, him to avoid upsetting me. I made sure he left before I did. He has no key so won't be here when I get back because I won't tell him when that is until it suits me.

I'm travelling first class. I've used my credit card knowing that I can't really afford it but I'll be able to pay it off when Adam's legacy comes through. Until then I'll just have to suffer the interest and hope for the best.

I used to travel off-peak cheapest when I visited him before. I've chosen off-peak again, but only because I don't want to rub shoulders with too many people.

The train to Paddington is full because it's the first off-peak train of the morning. But in first class, it's fine. No one is sitting next to me. I've chosen a window seat, prebooked. I debated whether it would be better to book an aisle seat and hope the window seat remained empty, then imagined someone sitting there, blocking my view. I considered a single seat on the other side of the aisle – the ones you only get in first class – both window and aisle seat, but dismissed it, eventually. I like the space a double seat with no companion gives me. I dump my wheelie case in the foot-space of the aisle seat; there's no prebooked ticket on it, so my case should deter anyone from joining me.

I realise I'm quite selfish.

The train pulls into Paddington and I decide to continue my extravagance and get a taxi to Adam's. Not that it is Adam's any longer. It's mine.

One of the very best things about having brothers who are solicitors is that they do all the legal stuff in our family, almost without thinking about it. Naturally Adam appointed them as executors to his will so all the messy stuff, the probate, all that, is already being handled by them. My brother George has said it will take quite a while to unravel Adam's finances as they are complex, and obviously he had a lot of money, so there will be inheritance tax to pay. He's made an appointment for me to see Adam's accountant and his financial advisor later this week. George mentioned something about irregularities; Maths was always Adam's forte so I can imagine his finances being creative but never dishonest.

My main job is to go through his belongings, his paintings – the ones in his studio – are all mine. But they have to be valued and included in his estate before I can sell them; I need to liaise with Jasper about that. George has given me a document with a timeline and a list of processes. I have to admit that my eyes glazed over when I saw it. What I do know is that it appears it will take a long time, too long.

He's also given me a new key because he had the locks changed two days after Adam's death. George doesn't really trust anyone outside family.

When I tumble out of the taxi outside Adam's building, dragging my case behind me, I stop to really take in the beauty of the place. It's old. Or at least the front façade is, carefully preserved to comply with some sort of conservation or preservation, or whatever it is, order. Inside is quite something else; ultra-modern.

'Ms Hames, so nice to see you again, even under these circumstances.' Martin, the concierge, rushes towards me after he's buzzed me through the main door, and takes my case from me. 'You will need to sign in,' he says, looking embarrassed.

'It's fine. I know all about that.'

Another one of George's instructions.

'I have been told that once you sign in for the first time you're free to come and go as you please. I understand you're now the new owner.'

'Yes.' I concentrate on signing my name in the book. It's leather bound and the paper is cream and thick. I've never seen this before as I've never signed in, just been waved in by Martin or one of the faceless others once Adam introduced me. It got so that I just wandered in and took the lift to the penthouse without Martin even calling up first.

Well, that's how it used to be before Perry.

'The post, it's been piling up a while.' Martin opens a little door behind him and lifts out Adam's post. When he passes it to me I just stuff it in the front pocket of my handbag. I can deal with that later, much later.

Martin wheels my case over to the lift, presses the button and waits for it to come.

'I can manage from here,' I say, fearing he might be planning on escorting me to the door.

'Of course,' he says, as the lift door opens and I step inside. He hands over my case and smiles.

Once I've played around getting Adam's door unlocked, I let it swing open by itself. I'm almost afraid to step inside. I imagine Adam here, teasing me, accusing me of being dramatic when we all know he's the dramatic one. I can hardly bear to go inside, yet I must. There's a note that's been pushed under the door from the cleaner explaining that since there's no answer she can't get in to clean. There's a phone number. I assume this was weeks ago, she must know by now that Adam is dead.

The place looks the same except it's untidy. For Adam, it's very untidy. Discarded clothes, empty glasses and cups scattered around. It's so unlike him. I know the police have been here, allegedly looking for clues. Not that they found any. I don't think they would have bothered at all if Jasper hadn't badgered them. I don't think I can blame the police for dirty cups and glasses, discarded clothes.

I wander around, open the fridge door.

'Argh.' I'm gagging. The smell is awful. There's something green and furry in a dish on the shelf. There're also a few other bits that actually look okay, but they'll all have to go in the bin.

I think I'll ring his cleaner later.

I go through to my bedroom, or at least the room I've always thought of as mine. It looks just the same.

I wander out to the terrace, grateful that Adam still kept the key in the door. The Thames looks its usual romantic self. I snigger at my own notion; how can a river be romantic? Yet it is. I take a deep breath before wandering back inside to finish my tour, my inspection.

Adam's bedroom. The bed unmade, unclean. I'm glad I won't be sleeping in here. I think of Adam and Perry in that bed and shudder.

The studio. Filled with paintings. He was working towards an exhibition. Though that time has been and gone now. Jasper has already been in touch to say that he'll sort out another as soon as I'm ready. Jasper's confident he'll get good prices; Adam's work now carries a premium because there won't be any more. He mentioned something about missing paintings which Adam said Perry must have taken.

A half-done canvas sits on the easel. The paints have now congealed and hardened on the palette. Adam's painting jacket is discarded on the back of a chair. It makes me catch my breath. He could just walk in at any moment, pull on the jacket, pick up a brush and paint. But he won't be doing that. I sit down on his chair and cry.

I'm glad I'm alone. I'm glad I didn't bring Gray.

The entry phone rings and I stumble out of the studio to answer it. I hope it's the cleaner dropping by on the off chance.

It's Martin. 'Ms Hames, I have a visitor for you.'

'Tell her it's Jasper,' Jasper calls.

'Send him up, please.'

I open the door to him.

He steps out of the lift, rushes forward and hugs me. 'Darling girl,' he says, his voice husky.

'I've just arrived, you were lucky to catch me. I thought I said I'd give you a ring to arrange a time to sort out the paintings.'

'I'm not here about the paintings. I overheard you telling your brother you'd be coming today. I took a chance. I wanted to see you. We haven't had a chance to talk properly since it happened.'

'No.'

'How is everything?' He glances around. 'Ah, just the same.'

'Same as when?'

'The day… it happened.'

'Of course, you were here.'

'Yes. I was worried about him. He rang me, although for a while he'd been acting irrationally, I thought. Did you know he sent me an email and sacked me, then denied it? Said he'd been hacked.'

I stare at him. Shake my head. 'Perry probably?'

He nods. 'I took Adam out to lunch.' He glances around again. 'After I'd made him shower and change. He really wasn't himself.' He stops. 'Do you mind if I get myself a glass of water?'

'No, feel free. I can't offer you anything else, oh, unless you're happy with black coffee?'

'Water is fine.' He strides over and runs the tap, hunts around for two glasses then brings them over. 'Should we sit down?'

We sit at the table, it's covered in bits of paper, an empty whisky bottle, a sticky glass. We push them aside.

'I told the police this but they weren't really very interested. Well, no, that's not fair, they weren't very forthcoming with me. Perhaps they've told you more?'

I shrug. 'George says there are irregularities. I'm seeing Adam's accountant this week.'

Jasper sighs.

'He rang me that day, left a garbled voicemail. I was in a stupid meeting about nothing special.' I stop speaking because tears are welling. 'By the time I rang him back it was too late. I didn't see your texts until it was too late either.'

'It wasn't your fault.'

'But if I'd answered that call maybe I could have stopped him doing it.'

'It really wasn't your fault.'

'How do *you* know? Maybe I could have talked him round.' I'll never stop blaming myself.

'Because I was with him. And, as I told the police, he wasn't suicidal. Down, yes, but that was because of *him*.'

'Perry.'

'Yes. That's why he rung you, so that you could confirm that Perry did exist.'

'What?'

'No one had ever met him. Perry had cleared out, disappeared, removed all traces. You had seen him on a video call, Adam said.'

I wait, not sure where this is leading.

'You did see him?'

I nod. 'Yes, I did. But in the distance. I couldn't see his face properly. I couldn't pick him out in a crowd of two. Except for the hair, maybe. So blond. Like an albino. But he wasn't, Adam said he had dark eyes. I think. *You* must have met him.'

'Never, not once. Anyway, on that day at lunch, Adam told me he thought he was going mad. Then he told me he'd given Perry large sums of money to buy a property, a flat, but he'd been there looking for Perry and no one knew of him.'

I can feel my face scrunching up in pain. 'The bastard scammed my brother. That's what you implied in one of your texts.'

'That was what we concluded at lunch. It took us a little while but yes, that was what we thought.'

'And the police?'

'I told them all this. I told your brother, George, too. The police said something about it taking a while to investigate a crime like this, if it was a crime because Adam had been very clear and determined to give Perry the money. He took out a massive mortgage on this place…'

'I know about that. It's part of why I have to sell it.

Not that I could afford to live here anyway. Not that I'd want to without Adam.'

'On that day, at lunch, after we'd worked it out, that he'd been scammed, he suddenly jumped up, muttered something about Perry then ran. I went after him but I had to pay for lunch, I just gave them my card and ran too. But, I'm not as young and fit as Adam was. Fortunately, he's quite distinctive and tall; I saw him disappear down the Underground stairs. From a distance I saw him leap the barrier. I got through because I have an Oyster card, but Adam hasn't.'

'No.' I smile. 'He didn't like roughing it.'

'Quite.' He swallows and he looks away. 'I was at the top of the stairs to the platform when it happened…'

I wait. I want to hear it. I don't want to hear it.

'He just lurched backwards.' Jasper shakes his head. 'In front of the train. It wasn't right. I told the police, it wasn't right. He wasn't suicidal.'

'They said no one else was involved. They checked the CCTV. They said they couldn't see that anyone else was involved.'

'I don't know how they could tell, that platform was so crowded. I don't believe he wanted to die. He was saying he was going to track Perry down. He called him a bastard. Adam wasn't suicidal.'

'But the police…'

'I know, I know. They told me too how no one was involved. I don't believe it, Angie. Perry is clever, very clever. Far too clever.'

Twenty-two

Jasper arranges for the paintings to be collected. The specialist couriers are in Adam's studio for a long time, wrapping and packaging, but finally, they're gone.

The meetings with Adam's accountant and financial advisor have not gone well. The accountant informed me that Adam has a sizeable tax bill to pay soon and the financial advisor seemed to be more interested in covering his own arse than helping. He kept saying that he'd warned Adam against cashing in his investments, he'd advised him to at least get his name on any property deeds. He has no idea where said property is, but thinks it might have been in Kensington. Although, as Jasper has said, Adam followed that up to no avail.

I've finally opened all Adam's post, there's a polite letter about his mortgage payment being overdue. I spent an hour on the phone explaining that Adam is dead, so now they've agreed to suspend it and wait for full repayment once the flat is sold. I have to provide the relevant documents, so I've handed that over to George.

This is all so unlike Adam. He never worried about finances because he always had more than enough money, but he wasn't stupid. He wasn't a fool.

Perry has made him a fool.

What with the tax bill and the mortgage I have no choice but to sell the apartment, not that I didn't already know that. I've had it valued and told it will sell quickly and I realise that I should have a sizeable sum left. Certainly enough to move out of my flat with the view of B&Q's loading bay. Not that there's anything wrong with my flat, it's nice and cosy. I could easily stay there. Maybe I could invest Adam's money and live off the interest – ironically his financial advisor suggested exactly that. But I don't think it will be enough to cover all my living costs. Not unless I can recover all of Adam's money.

I'd much rather Adam was alive and well and I wasn't dealing with all this.

I'm really annoyed with him for getting himself conned like this.

I've spoken to the police and so has George regarding Adam's money, they're still investigating; it could be months and months, it could be fruitless. The bank account Adam transferred the money into has already been closed. And, as they pointed out, he transferred the money himself, and not just once. It wasn't the normal online scam. They seemed to be implying it wasn't a scam at all but something else altogether. The phrase money laundering wasn't mentioned but it felt implied.

It's taking me a long time to empty Adam's flat. I can't bear to get rid of his things, even though I know I must. I've sold his rather expensive dining table and chairs and his bed so far. That's it and I've been up here for two weeks. I need a break and I'll come back in a week or two.

Gray has messaged or rung me every day, offering to join me, offering support. He's being sweet, I know that. When I finally tell him I'm coming home he sounds elated. He's picking me up from the station, which means he'll be running me home, which means he'll probably expect to stay the night.

I think I might let him. I've actually missed having him around.

He's standing in the station forecourt as I head towards the exit turnstiles. He really is very attractive, other women, even some men, give him a second look. His hair has grown since I first met him, he'd had it cropped very short then because he said it was hot out in Dubai where he was working. Now he's moved back to the UK permanently, he says he'll let it grow a little longer. His hair is dark and rather luxurious. He sees me, waves and smiles.

Once I'm through the ticket barrier he hurries towards me and hugs me, burying his face in my hair.

'I've missed you,' he says.

'Me too,' I mutter. I'd really rather not be having this affectionate display out in public. 'Shall we go?'

'Yes, absolutely. Are you hungry?'

'A bit.' I am but I don't want to go to a restaurant.

'Great, because I've got all the ingredients to cook something lovely for supper while you relax in the bath.' He links my arm and escorts me to his car.

'Okay.' Is he implying I smell? I'm not going to take offence; he's being kind.

I don't have a bath, I don't want one, I don't need one, instead I chill with a glass of wine or two while he cooks for us. It's something that involves frying meat and making sauces, and he seems to be enjoying himself.

He puts the food on the table and while he doesn't actually say, 'ta da,' it's implied.

'Looks fab,' I say, genuinely impressed and certainly finding I do have quite an appetite.

'Thank you.'

We tuck in, the silence broken only by the sound of us eating and me making suitably appreciative sounds. It is good, it's very good, he's a good cook.

'How was it at your brother's place?'

I grimace a little and shake my head. I really don't want to talk about Adam or the mess he's left behind. And I definitely don't want to talk about Adam my darling little brother.

I change the subject. 'I have a doctor's appointment tomorrow. I'm going to get my sick leave extended.'

'Good idea. You do have a lot to deal with.'

I nod my agreement. He's right, I do, and he doesn't know the half of it, very little in fact. My brother's death has knocked me for six, I miss him so much it's a physical ache that never goes away. I don't know if it ever will. But the financial mess he left behind is bewildering.

'Do you mind if I don't ask you to stay the night?' I ask Gray, once he's finished clearing up.

He stares at me for a second or two, probably wondering at the cheek of me, letting him cook and clean up before dropping my bombshell. But just because he's made dinner doesn't mean I have to sleep with him. 'Of course,' he says. 'It's been a tough old time for you. I'll get off shortly. You just call if you want me.'

'Thank you,' I say, my voice its sweetest. 'And thank you for the lovely meal.'

He looks genuinely pleased to be complimented. 'My pleasure.'

After he's gone, having assured me he'll ring in the morning – I wish he wouldn't – I slowly unpack my case and put my clothes away. Hardly anything is dirty because I used Adam's washing machine; it's better than mine. It's top of the range so I think I might keep it, sell my own. There are a couple of other things I want to keep too, the rest I'll offer to the family and what's left can be sold or donated to charity. I'd love to keep his sofas but they're far too large for my place. And, I suspect, I won't be moving any time soon.

☯☯☯

Gray rang early this morning, he wanted me to come and spend a day out with him. Says it would be good for me, take my mind off things. I really don't feel very sociable at the moment and declined. I had to get quite forceful and in the end I told him I was having bad period pains – that always shuts men up, even Adam wouldn't argue with that – so really wasn't feeling like it. He gave in gracefully then, asked if I needed anything, so I told him what I really needed was peace and quiet and a long lie in.

Liar.

Gray reminded me that I had a doctor's appointment and suggested I mention my painful periods while I was there. I didn't quite laugh out loud; he obviously isn't very experienced with women and their workings.

While I was at Adam's I did a bit of research on Perry. I couldn't find anyone who'd actually met him. Martin, the concierge, said that one of the agency concierges had seen him but they'd had no luck tracking him down. It appears Adam had instructed Martin to check it out. He said that Adam seemed to be wondering if he'd imagined Perry and that's why he was so desperate to find anyone who'd met him in person.

I've spoken to Jasper a lot lately, too. What he said backed that up, telling me about deleted photos on Adam's phone. I still feel guilty for not being able to take

Adam's call that day. It breaks my heart every time I think of it.

I've been on Perry's website, the one Adam showed me. It looks genuine. I sent them a message via their contact form. I had to be careful about what I said, so kept it simple, saying that I needed to contact Perry Oblekt and that it was personal and a matter of urgency. That was three days ago and so far, no reply. I wonder if there's a phone number I could call?

Maybe it's a fake website. Given how Perry has gone to ground nothing would surprise me.

I fire up my laptop – my intention to attempt more internet searching on Perry, so much easier than on my phone – when an email pops up. It's from Perry's company. Yes!

Dear Ms Hames
Per Oblekt (not Perry) says he has no recollection of you. Please could you explain the matter further.
Kind regards
Olga Henson

Great, what the hell can I say? I close my laptop and flick on the TV. I'm just settling into something easy and silly when my phone rings. It's an estate agent, about selling Adam's flat.

'Ms Hames, may I call you Angie? It's Doug here from…'

'Hi,' I say, forcing a smile onto my face.

'Yes, as you know we valued your brother's apartment last week, and although you haven't instructed us to put it on the market yet, I do have someone who is interested in viewing it.'

I'm silent, probably for too long. The reality of selling

Adam's home is hitting me hard.

'Angie?'

'Yes, sorry, right…'

'Obviously they'd like to see it but they're very keen, been after a place in that building for a few years now.' I can tell from his tone that he's grinning to himself. 'Perhaps they could pop round today for a viewing?'

'No, not today. I'm not there at the moment. I don't live in London, you see. I'm back in my home town.'

'Ah, I see. Perhaps you would like to leave a key with us so we can arrange viewings?' His voice sounds so hopeful.

'But I haven't instructed you yet. There may be other agents with better deals. I haven't decided who I'm going with.' It seems I am a proper liar today because they were the only agent I've called so far. I found the whole thing so traumatic that I couldn't bear to repeat it just yet.

'Well, Ms Hames, Angie, if this client decides to buy your brother's apartment we could come to an arrangement on our terms. Since we won't have to advertise it, which is of course better from your perspective too given the circumstances, our costs will be reduced.'

'Okay…'

We discuss it further and in the end I agree to go up tomorrow and be there for the viewing. Under no circumstances am I handing over the key to anyone. Apart from my own reluctance to do that, big brother George would kill me.

If I sell Adam's place soon it does solve a lot of problems, it'll pay off the mortgage and the outstanding, and still growing, bills – who knew the maintenance charges in that block were so high? It would also pay off the gargantuan credit card bill that arrived yesterday morning, handed to me by Martin and which I only opened this morning. I knew Adam had a gold card with a high limit but he said he never used it. Yet it's full of flights and hotels, shopping in Harrods, and even jewellery purchases.

I don't think Adam used it at all.

I think Perry might have.

Twenty-three

I buy the cheapest train ticket I can get to London. How different this journey feels to my last one.

I'm still reeling from the shock of the credit card bill; I cannot believe it. I just know that Adam didn't run up a bill like that, he just wouldn't. As well as Perry scamming all of Adam's investment money and tricking him into taking out a mortgage, he's been using his credit card to fund all these *love* trips. Adam couldn't believe how generous Perry was, always refusing to allow Adam to pay for anything, now I know why.

I'm settled in a seat nudged up to the window by a large, slightly sweaty man when the train pulls out. I get my phone out and check for messages. Inevitably there's one from Gray. He wanted to visit me last night but I put him off again. I told him that I planned to go up to London again today and he said he wanted to come too. He says he's worried about me and he thinks I'm overdoing it. He's really rather sweet. I'm glad I didn't dump him after the funeral. However, there are some things I want to do alone. And I'm not staying overnight, I'll be on a train home as soon as this viewing is over.

Martin greets me when I enter the building then holds up a finger suggesting I wait a moment. He produces more post addressed to Adam. My heart sinks, I hope there are no more bills.

Once in the apartment I open the post. A letter, actually addressed to me, from the bank confirming our arrangements, a reminder from the credit card company that last month's payment has not been made. I suppose I'll have to ring them to explain the situation; but at least there are no new horrors.

Adam's home is looking less like his home than ever now. The place is immaculately clean – thanks to his cleaner – and with some large items of furniture now sold, it's looking bare, including the fridge, now fresh and empty.

The entry phone rings and Martin announces that the estate agent is downstairs with two other people.

'Send them up,' I tell him.

In the few minutes it takes them to come up in the lift my mind starts working overtime. What if the potential buyer is Perry, fronting it out safe in the knowledge that I won't know him? I'm almost hyperventilating at the idea of it when there's a knock at the door.

Doug stands before me as I gingerly open it. Then he introduces his clients, Mr and Mrs Shah. I'm so relieved that I grin inanely. There is no way this middle-aged Asian couple can be Perry in disguise.

They wander around while I stand near the bifold doors staring out at the Thames. I'll miss this view, but not as much as I'm missing Adam. I catch my breath at the thought of him. My little bro.

'Beautiful, isn't it?' Mrs Shah says, standing next to me and staring out too.

'It is. Even more so at night when the lights twinkle.'

'I can imagine.'

Mr Shah joins us, standing next to his wife and giving her an almost imperceptible nod. She nods back.

'We'd like to make you an offer,' he says. 'Full asking price.'

'Umm, well…'

Doug steps forward. 'I think we should let Ms Hames consider the offer on her own.' He attempts to usher the Shahs out, and though they do go, they seem reluctant.

An hour later, just as I'm settling into the train seat on my return journey, my phone rings. It's Doug.

'Have you had time to consider the Shahs' offer? Only they've upped the offer by twenty-five thousand,' he says, barely able to contain his glee.

'What?' I'm truly shocked. Isn't getting the asking price the best you can expect? Yet here these people are offering even more and there's no other party involved, they're bidding against themselves.

'Twenty-five thousand more?' I repeat.

'I'm sure I could push them for more. They're so keen. They love the place.'

It's tempting but that would be pure greed on my part. The extra twenty-five will make a fair dent in the credit card bill.

'Tell them I accept and I hope they'll be very happy there.'

I've just arrived home when my phone rings again. It's Doug. I'm tempted not to answer, but that is just being silly.

'They want all the furniture,' he says, sounding so pleased with himself. 'They're also interested in the car.'

'What car?'

'The one in the parking bay.'

'Oh, yes.' I haven't even looked at Adam's car. It's not

much use to me, I couldn't afford the insurance. I'll need to clear it out first though.

'None of that is included in the price.'

'I told them that. They said they'd be happy to take everything just as it is, including all the white goods, and offer you another ten thousand for the furniture and whatever the retail value is of the car.'

'I'll have to think about it,' I tell him. I need to check what I could get for those sofas; and I haven't even offered them to any of my brothers.

Gray rings ten minutes later for an update. When I tell him it's sold, he says that we should celebrate. I tell him I don't feel like celebrating. I don't. How can I? So he suggests I come over to his and he'll look after me. I remind him that I won't be having sex with him tonight. He laughs and assures me that much as he'd love to have sex with me it's not all I'm good for.

I message the family group and tell them the news. Then I offer them the sofas or anything else they might want.

Grace comes back and asks for Adam's art stuff for her daughter, Ellie. She's just started A level art and Grace thinks Ellie might have inherited some of Adam's talent. We can but hope, and of course she can have his stuff. I warn her there's a lot of it.

No one wants the sofas. I wonder what their real worth is? Are they just second-hand sofas or are they vintage masterpieces? The irony isn't lost on me that Perry would probably know.

Which reminds me that I still haven't replied to the email from Perry's website. Although, of course, it's not Perry's website, of that I am sure. I just have enough time before Gray picks me up. I pull out my laptop.

It takes me several attempts with much typing and

deleting before I am reasonably satisfied with the result. Surely this will elicit some response.

Dear Ms Henson
My brother was in a relationship with Perry Oblekt. I believe it may be possible that Perry Oblekt is pretending to be Per Oblekt. He certainly shows people your company website and passes it off as his own. Since my brother has now died in suspicious circumstances and Perry has vanished, we are trying to ascertain the truth.
Yours hopefully
Angie Hames

I grit my teeth; press send and slap the laptop shut. Just then a knock on the door tells me that Gray has arrived.

He hugs and kisses me and it feels good. It's nice to have someone on my side, someone who really cares for me. I know I have my family but they're busy with their own families, even my parents are, understandably, wrapped up in themselves. Our mum's grief is so palpable that she's as fragile as glass. Although she denies it Adam was always her favourite; the baby that should never have been.

'Congratulations on selling Adam's place so quickly.'

I shrug. 'It sold itself really. They fell in love with it, especially that view over the river.'

'Of course. It is stunning, especially at night. Shall we go?'

I've only been to Gray's place twice before. On both occasions we had both had a few drinks and had fallen into bed kissing and giggling. There won't be any giggling tonight.

It's an odd place, a three-bed modern detached house

on an estate. Very nice but it's not him, not at all. It's rented and was fully furnished when he moved in. He says it's very temporary but is fine until he decides to buy. When he left Dubai he sold off most of his possessions, especially furniture as he said the cost of shipping it back here was prohibitive. Anyway, he says it will be fun choosing new.

He cooks a lovely meal for us then we settle down and watch TV before I fall asleep on his shoulder. I wake up with neck ache.

'Hello sleepy,' he says.

'Sorry. What time is it? I need to go.' I start looking round for my coat, my bag.

'Stay.'

I frown.

'I promise I won't molest you.' He kisses me softly on the top of my head.

'Okay,' I say, but only because it's cold outside and I'm tired.

☯☯☯

The next morning he drops me off home on his way to work. I'm not really sure what it is he does only that it has something to do with oil and insurance. To be honest I don't really care. He has talked about his job, about his life in Dubai, about how despite having a few relationships he'd never found the one to settle down with, grow old with. Whatever his job is it's obviously well paid because he's shown me a few photographs of his place in Dubai and it's amazing, better even than Adam's place.

'Shall I come round tonight after work?' he asks.

'Okay.' I grin. 'I'll get us a takeaway, any preference?'

'Thai,' he says, laughing.

It's later in the day when I'm checking my emails that the reply from Per Oblekt's company comes through. It's polite and short and very to the point saying that Per has not been out of Sweden in years as he has an illness which makes travel very difficult. Also attached is a short biography for him, obviously the sort of thing used for press releases. Among other things it's gives his date of birth and I easily work out that he's seventy-nine. There's also a recent photo of an old man.

Suspicion is right, Perry is an imposter.

I think I was always suspicious of him.

Shame Adam hadn't been.

Twenty-four

Two months later

"I've just got a text. We're exchanging contracts today,' I tell Gray. We're lying in his bed, snuggled up.

'Excellent. When are you completing?'

'Two weeks or so, I think. Up to the Shahs, makes no difference to me.'

He leans over and kisses me on the nose. 'I need to get ready for work,' he says, sighing. 'Hate leaving you.'

Our relationship has grown warm and loving. He's helped me a lot over Adam's loss. He's kind and understanding and now that I can accept his sympathy he's been an amazing support. He's even encouraged me to jack in my job because, as he pointed out, I can live on what Adam has left me until I can find a job I love. There really is no rush. I haven't given my notice yet because I'm still officially on sick leave. But that will end in a few weeks and then it will be decision time. But for now I'm just living in the moment. Those moments are good when I'm with Gray.

I've even told him all about the Per/Perry situation. He was absolutely horrified and so supportive. I told Jasper too, not that it came as a shock to him, not really.

He saw far more of Adam during the Perry months than I did. He said he could see that Adam wasn't truly himself, especially towards the end.

I've contacted the police too; they've logged what I've said. They say they haven't been able to trace the money yet – I suspect they're not really trying. They say the fraud case remains open but not Adam's death as there is no evidence to suggest it was anything other than either an accident or suicide. The coroner returned an open verdict.

I feel sick when I think about Adam's money. Then I feel guilty for worrying about it. Yes, I'll receive a nice amount when the apartment is sold but that's not the point. When I think of how hard Adam worked, how talented and clever he was, how every penny he had he earned and how generous he was, I want revenge.

A part of me wants to find Perry and punish him.

Some hope of that.

'I was thinking,' Gray says a few days after I've exchanged on Adam's place.

'Did it hurt,' I joke.

He grins. 'No seriously. I was thinking, would you fancy Christmas in Dubai?'

I stare at him. I'm puzzled, confused.

'What?' he says, frowning at me.

'Christmas. I always spend Christmas with my family. It's loud and noisy and we eat and drink too much but it's… Christmas. It's tradition.'

'So break with tradition,' he says.

'I don't think it would go down well.'

'Whyever not?'

I shrug. It's true it won't be the same this year because Adam won't be there, doling out quirky gifts and a lot of affection. It won't feel right without him but surely my absence too would make the situation worse. Especially for my parents. My mum is a shadow of herself, so thin I swear I can count her ribs through her clothes.

'What do *you* normally do?' I ask him.

'Spend it somewhere hot and sunny,' he says, with a laugh. 'I was living in Dubai for the last ten Christmases, there's so much to do, places to go, things to see.'

'Right.'

'Don't worry if you don't fancy it. I just thought it would be nice to go somewhere warm and bright, that's all.'

'Probably too hot for me anyway.'

'Oh no, it's not super-hot in December. Just a nice temperature. You'd love it. Why don't you have a think about it. It's a while off, we don't have to decide now.'

'No. Okay,' I agree, but I've already decided, I'm not going to Dubai for Christmas. My family needs me. And I need my family.

☯☯☯

I can leave it no longer; I have to go to London today and remove the final few items of Adam's from his apartment. The Shahs are having most of the furniture right down to pots and pans which is a great help; my niece has had his painting bits; we went up together and packed it up to be couriered back to her. All I'm checking for is personal items, that means going through the kitchen drawers – who knows what could be lurking in the corners.

And I haven't come across yin yet. I know it's there somewhere, definitely in a drawer, tossed carelessly and with laughter when I took yang up. I really need to find yin even if it means crawling on the floor looking under the sofas.

'I can easily take some time off work,' Gray says, as he dresses for work.

'No, there's no need. Up and down in a day. Just picking up a few bits.' I also have to leave the keys with the estate agents and, under George's instructions, I have to tell Martin that no one is allowed in there until he rings to advise the sale has completed and the money has all come through.

The train journey seems to go on for ever. It's raining when I finally reach Paddington and I decide to take a taxi because I will be able to easily afford it soon. Anyway, since I've not been going to work I've actually saved money because they're still paying me while I'm off sick and I haven't really been out much spending money.

When the taxi pulls up outside Adam's building, I fight the urge to cry. This is the last time I will ever visit here, ever stand on that balcony terrace and stare at the river. This is severing my last bond with Adam and his life in London.

Martin greets me as I go in and I'm soon in the lift and on my way.

Adam's apartment is cold and unlived in. I've never seen it like this. The heating hasn't been on for weeks, so I find the controller and turn it up high. I may not be staying long but I cannot bear being this cold. Also, it'll air the place a bit for the new owners.

I wander through the rooms. Adam's studio is just a shell now, empty, cavernous, bright even on a dull day like today. The paintings went several months ago, they're safe in Gerard's store waiting to be displayed. He's holding Adam's posthumous show starting mid-December. He's expecting great prices. The money will all come to me and I wonder if I should have waited to see if it was enough to pay off the mortgage. But the reality is that even if that is the case – unlikely – I could never have afforded to run the apartment the way Adam did. I could never afford to live in it. I would have had to rent it out and what would be the point in that? Also, the inheritance tax will be due as well as Adam's final personal tax bill.

I hate Perry Oblekt, or whatever his real name is.

Adam's bedroom has only the built-in furniture left, the wardrobes and bedside drawers. I check each methodically. All emptied. I enlisted the help of his cleaner and it was her who took his clothes away, not that Adam was very interested in clothes, and she cleaned out every cupboard in this room.

If I don't find yin today I must ask her if she's seen it. I hope she hasn't thrown it away.

Next I check the spare room, my room. The bed is the same, although it's been stripped. The wardrobe is empty, but it always was, ditto the bedside drawers. I used to just live out of my case when I came on my weekend visits. All that seems so long ago.

The living room sounds echoey and looks bare. I've taken the big, fluffy rug that covered the floor between the sofas. How often we sat with our bare feet on it, laughing and joking and drinking wine. There's a tell-tale stain as proof, albeit a small one. Adam did that. It wasn't his wine; it was mine but *he* knocked it over, fortunately it was a rosé and not a red. We argued about the waste of wine versus the damage done to the rug. The stain is tiny and faint but I'll never have it removed now; it's an indelible memory. The rug is rolled up in the hallway of my place; I don't know what to do with it now.

I check all the bathroom cabinets, both bathrooms.

Nothing.

Then I go through the kitchen cupboards and drawers, slowly, methodically. I find an old takeaway menu and a receipt for a pair of shoes, expensive pink loafers, don't remember seeing those when we cleared his stuff out and not really his style. Maybe he bought them for Perry. There's nothing else, just a dinner service, plain white because Adam didn't like over-decorated things. He liked plain, which is odd given how vibrant his paintings were.

I've found nothing. It's hands and knees time now.

Where is yin?

The state of the floor is a testament to his cleaner's efficiency. Even after crawling around on my hands and knees to peer under the sofas, my trousers are still clean. I can't see anything under there. I wanted to move them but they're just too heavy.

So that's it, no yin.

I text the cleaner just in case she's seen it, or thrown it away. I'll be sad if that's the case but at least I'll know.

She texts back to say she's never seen a little white stone in the shape of a comma.

I'm trying to remember where he found it again in the first place. Was it the sideboard? It's still here, the new owners are buying that too. I pull out the drawers in the middle, completely remove them. They're empty but my last hope is that the space below might hold something. It does. Another takeaway menu.

But no yin.

One last check of his car. Although I have cleared it out – not that it was messy – I didn't check under the seats, yin could have fallen down there.

But it hasn't. Definitely no yin.

I have to go. I have to drop the keys off and then

catch my train home. I feel so sad about yin. Stupid really.

Martin comes out from behind his desk and hugs me as I leave. We both have tears in our eyes.

'End of an era,' he says, stepping back and nipping behind his desk.

I remind him that no one can enter the flat until my brother rings to confirm the sale has gone through. He gives me a knowing nod.

Then I'm out of there.

☯☯☯

Back home I rummage in one of my handbags until I find yang, still there from the last time I took it to show Adam. It's so upsetting yet I feel silly for being so upset; it's just a stone.

Gray is on his way round; he says he's bringing food to cook. I'm really not hungry but he'll cook it anyway.

'How did it go,' he asks, grimacing at me. He can see my red-rimmed eyes no doubt.

'Oh, you know. It's sad. I'm sad. I'm going to miss that place.' That sounds so bad I almost wince, but Gray doesn't pick up on it. While I still had the apartment I could pretend Adam was still alive, just off somewhere for a few months. Once it's gone…

'Yes, I can imagine you'll miss the view from that terrace and across the Thames, the lights twinkling at night.'

'I will.'

'Come on, sit down and let me look after you. I'm going to cook something quick and simple. I'm starving. But first, let's have a drink.' He pulls out a bottle of wine and I don't bother putting up a fight when he pours me a large glass. I might just as well drown my sorrows.

‘Have you thought any more about Dubai?’ he asks, as he starts chopping and frying things.

I blink several times before I answer. I thought I’d already said no but maybe I wasn’t forceful enough.

‘It’s out of the question. There’ll be a big Adam shaped hole at the heart of our family and I can’t make that even bigger by being absent.’

He glances up from his chopping and frying. ‘Okay,’ he says. ‘Maybe next year.’

Twenty-five

'You're still looking glum,' Gray says, a few days later.

We're lounging around at his place and I have to admit that I am feeling glum. But I don't think that's unreasonable. I don't answer him.

'What you need is cheering up.'

'Do you think?' I don't mean that to sound so sarcastic.

'Try looking on the bright side. Any day now you'll get the money from the sale of Adam's flat and you won't have any money worries again, possibly ever.'

I snort. 'It's not that much,' I say. Anyway, having lots of money hasn't saved Adam, has it? Quite the opposite.

Gray has no idea how much money I'm getting because I've never told him. There have been a few times when he's looked as though he was going to ask, but hasn't. Since Adam's flat was never advertised Gray doesn't know what the asking price was. All he does know it that there's a mortgage to be paid off and other debts before I get anything. He doesn't know much about Adam's place because he's never seen it and I haven't talked about it much, not the detail anyway. I find it too painful. So he really knows nothing.

I shudder. All this talk, this thought of money, it's so

distasteful.

'Angie.' Gray puts his arm around me. 'Your brother would want you to enjoy what he's left you. He worked hard for it and now you'll benefit. It's obviously what he wanted.'

'I think Adam didn't envisage me having his money quite so soon.' I shrug Gray off and excuse myself to go to the loo.

When I come back he's grinning. Sometimes I can't decide if Gray is insensitive or stupid. Maybe it's hard for him to understand how close we were, he has no siblings, no family to speak of at all since both his parents are long dead. And yet he's been so supportive during all this. Perhaps I've oversensitive. He's staring at me.

'What?' I realise he's been talking but I haven't heard a word.

'I said I've booked us a treat.'

'Which is?'

'A weekend away.'

'Oh.'

'Bath. We can take in a bit of culture and chillax.'

'Oh.' I hate the word chillax, but the thought is kind.

'I think it'll be a nice diversion for you. You've had a rough old few months. It'll help. Are you excited?'

'Um, I suppose so.' I really don't have the energy for jaunts anywhere, let alone cultural ones.

'Good. I've booked a lovely hotel right in the centre.'

'When are we going?' Maybe by the time it comes around I will be feeling more inclined to enjoy it.

'At the weekend. Friday, straight after I finish work.'

'This weekend?'

He grins at me, then hugs me a bit too tightly. 'It's going to be great,' he says. 'Have you ever been to Bath?'

'Yeah, school trip and hen parties.'

'It'll be better than that.'

☯☯☯

Here we are, Friday, and I've painted on my jolly face and I'm making an effort, because, as Gray says, moping won't bring Adam back.

I know that.

He's driving, which is nice for me, I can just lie back and enjoy the journey. It should only take about an hour to get there.

The hotel is right in the centre and it's lovely; five stars, not that I would have expected anything less from Gray. We arrive in time for dinner which he says we should have in the hotel because it has a Michelin star. I agree because really, food isn't that important to me. I like eating but I don't really care what it is, within reason. Adam used to tell me I had an uneducated palate. I used to tease him back – this from the man whose favourite eatery was only one step up from a greasy spoon.

We return to our room after dinner; Gray has suggested a club he knows but I've declined that suggestion. I'm tired and just want to sleep.

We do the tourist things on Saturday and of course we go shopping. It is nice, Bath, and Gray is right I do feel distracted, which makes me feel better.

So Gray's not insensitive at all, he actually knows what's good for me.

'I've had a lovely day,' I tell him, throwing our shopping bags on the enormous bed and collapsing alongside them.

'It's not over yet,' he says. 'Have a bath and chillax, then get your glad rags on. We're going out.'

'Not clubbing,' I say. I never thought I'd say that, not

me, I was the original party girl every weekend with Adam. He couldn't keep up with me.

'No, just dinner, but somewhere special.'

The restaurant is special, it's stunning. It's also one of those places that doesn't show the prices on the menu. I've been to one or two of those before with Adam. It's not too large and there is plenty of space between the tables. It means no one can overhear others' conversations unless they zone in and stare in an obvious manner, and this place is too classy for that.

I'm glad I'm wearing one of my gorgeous new dresses, it's one I had doubts about but Gray convinced me I looked amazing in it. I feel amazing here, now. Anything less and I would be underdressed. Gray is wearing a suit, but no tie; as he said, no one wears a tie now except to funerals.

The food is served in minute portions on giant white plates. My choice mentioned asparagus but I can see none, just a swirl of green liquid decorating the plate.

'Is that the asparagus?' I giggle as I ask Gray.

He leans over and dips his finger in, then licks it. I'm amused and shocked in equal measure. 'Yep,' he says, grinning.

Even though we've had five courses, including cheese and biscuits, I don't feel overfull because of the minute portion size.

The waiter brings some kind of sweet liqueur in tiny glasses then fades away discreetly.

Gray reaches over and takes my hand. 'Have you enjoyed this evening?'

'Yes, I have and, if I'm honest, I wasn't in the mood for it.'

'I know what's best for you,' he says, grinning. I think the liqueur might be going to his head, that and the whole bottle of Barolo he's drunk almost to himself. I'm not a big lover of red wine, it's too earthy and heavy. Adam always called me a lightweight. But I've had a quarter of a glass just to keep Gray company. I didn't want a bottle, or even a glass of something different just for me.

'You look particularly beautiful tonight.'

'You too,' I say, laughing. 'Nice suit. Is it new? Did you buy it today?' I'm wondering if I could have been so focused on myself while shopping that I didn't notice. Surely not.

'It is new, but no, I brought it with me.'

I nod, relieved that I'm not so inattentive after all.

'I wanted to wear it,' he continues, 'because tonight is a special night.'

'Is it?' Is it his birthday? I hope it's not. But how was I to know if he never told me?

He dips his hand into his pocket then pulls out a tiny box.

My heart momentarily stops then restarts much faster. Is that what I think it is?

'My darling Angelique, will you do me the honour of being my wife?' He flips the box open to display a stunning and giant, diamond ring.

For a moment I just stare at him, at the ring.

I'm aware that the restaurant has become silent. I glance around and see that everyone is staring at us.

'Um, yes, of course.' I smile. But what else can I say? This is so public. So humiliating.

I've never seriously thought about marrying, having children, all that jazz. I always imagined growing old with Adam, the spinster sister and the bachelor brother, white haired and doddering around together. Adam knocking out the odd painting to keep us in style and me lying around watching TV and eating organic chocolate. That was my future, in my head, never discussed with Adam obviously. I always assumed that we would both have dalliances with men, but nothing would ever come of them.

Then Adam got engaged to Perry.

It felt like such a betrayal on so many levels. I know finding a boyfriend had been my idea but why did he have to go to such extremes? And Perry has turned out to be a thieving little shit which only makes the betrayal worse. I'm still angry with Adam for being so gullible, for locking me out. I'm sure ten minutes in Perry's company would have been enough for me to suss him out.

Gray is saying something. I smile again, because I haven't been listening.

'I hope it fits you, I had to guess your size because you don't wear rings so you didn't leave one lying around that I could measure.' He gives me a nervous smile.

'No.' Because I don't really like rings, but I can hardly say that. I hold out my hand and Gray squidges the ring onto my finger. It fits remarkably well. 'It's gorgeous.' I turn my hand around, letting the light catch the stone.

A bottle of champagne arrives, a gift from the restaurant. I almost gag at the prospect of having to drink half. Gray sees the look on my face and a little frown plays across his. He reaches for my hand again.

'Don't worry, we'll share it out.'

An hour later and we finally exit the place. Everyone claps as we stand. I'm just glad this isn't in our home town and no one knows me. Gray evidently doesn't know me as well as he thinks he does; I really don't like this level of showiness.

Back at the hotel I spend far too long in the bathroom, removing my clothes, removing my makeup, cleaning my teeth too forcefully.

Gray's waiting for me in bed. He looks happy, excited, expectant.

'I've got such a headache,' I lie, as I fall into bed beside him.

'Oh. I expect it's the excitement.'

'Probably.' I hold up the ring to the light, it is a stunner. 'Do you mind if we just go to sleep now?'

'Of course,' he says, turning out his bedside light.

We lie there in the darkness, neither of us asleep while I rewrite my plan for the future, a one that includes Gray.

Not Adam.

Twenty-six

I spent most of last night lying still and thinking.

I've weighed up the pros and cons. And the pros have won. Gray is good looking, very good looking in fact, and the squint rarely shows unless he's very tired, so no one other than me is going to see that. He's comfortably off financially. He's been exceptionally supportive during this tough time since Adam's death.

And he wants to marry me.

I can see a future for us. A family maybe if that's what he wants, a nice home. I'm not ready for all that just yet, maybe in a few years. But I can envisage it happening. That's my new future now, with Gray, not Adam.

'What do you want to do today?' he asks over breakfast, which he's had delivered to the room. So thoughtful of him.

'I don't mind. The Roman Baths maybe.'

'Great. I thought that too but didn't want to pressure you. How are you feeling now?' This is the third or fourth time he's asked me this morning. Previously I've just said okay.

'I feel great. That breakfast has really perked me up.'

We do the Roman Baths, we take a late, light lunch and then he drives us home. He expects me to stay at his place overnight and it would be churlish of me not to. He has an early start for work tomorrow. I, fortunately, don't.

I've been thinking,' he says, when we're snuggled up in bed, basking in that lovely post lovemaking glow. Gray really is the best lover I've ever had. In fact, if I think about him objectively, he's quite the catch in so many ways.

'Yes…'

'Now we're engaged why don't you move in here with me permanently?'

'But this isn't your permanent home. You could move in with me.' Not that I really want that.

'Your place is too small for both of us. Yes, this place is only rented, but we can go house hunting *together* now.'

'Yes, I suppose.'

'I'd like us to get married soon.' He sits up in bed as though a light has suddenly come on in his head. 'I wonder if we could arrange a Christmas wedding? What do you think? That would cheer everyone up, wouldn't it? Your family would love that.'

I'm stunned. 'There's no rush,' I say, trying to sound casual. He's right though, it would cheer up my family – some good news after so much bad.

'No. Of course. I was getting carried away there. It's just that now I've found you, now you've agreed to be my wife, I just want us to get on with our life together. This time next year we might even hear the patter of tiny feet.' He grins at me.

I don't reply. I'm too taken aback to say anything. Last night I just managed to convince myself that my future lay with Gray but I wasn't expecting it to start immediately.

'It's a lot to plan,' I say. 'By Christmas, I mean.'

'Yes, of course.' He looks crestfallen. 'But we don't want anything elaborate or extravagant, do we? That would be disrespectful to your brother.'

'Mmm. Maybe.' Am I agreeing or just playing for time?

'Let's see. It might be too soon.' He's reading me correctly. 'But in the meantime you should think about moving in with me and putting your place up for sale.'

'I'll give it some thought,' I say, meaning I will but not for quite some time. This is all happening far too fast for me.

Gray turns his back on me and I lie there with the covers pulled up as high as possible. Soon he's asleep, snoring gently, not too irritating.

A Christmas wedding? I turn the idea around in my head. No, it's far too soon and Christmas is just around the corner. I need time, downtime, on my own time.

I'm actually glad he's away for work most of this week.

☯☯☯

He's up early, creeping around as he gets ready for work and his trip and trying not to disturb me. But I'm a light sleeper and I'm fully awake the minute he slithers out of bed. I'm currently pretending otherwise because I don't want to have too much conversation before he leaves.

After a while he disappears off to the kitchen and I assume he's eating his breakfast. When he comes back in I shake myself awake and sit up.

'Morning, beautiful,' he says, a bright smile on his face.

'Hi.' I'm not at my best in the morning, though I think he probably knows this by now. I also have the makings of a headache.

He pulls a bag out and hurriedly packs enough clothes for his trip. Men are lucky, aren't they? A business trip means clean shirts and underwear, plus a shaver and toothbrush. Almost anything else they can make do, use what's in the hotel, not like us women.

'I'm leaving in a minute,' he says, zipping up his bag.

'Okay.'

'Are you going to stay here all week? If so, you'll need to get some food in.' He grins at me.

'Maybe.' Most certainly not. 'I need to go to my place for stuff…' I say vaguely.

'Well you know you're welcome here. Give my suggestion some more thought. I'd love you to move in permanently now. I think your place would sell really quickly, then we could get on with finding our forever home.'

I nod. Although I've already given it plenty of thought during the night. And it's too soon for selling my place yet.

He kisses and hugs me goodbye, then he's gone.

This place is pleasant enough, especially for a rental. It must be expensive, but it's impersonal. It came fully furnished and although the furniture is smart it's lifeless, hotel-like. Even the pictures on the wall are the sort you see in hotels. My place may not be smart but it's home. Anyway, I'm missing the sight of the B&Q loading bay. I laugh to myself; it could almost be true. I'm going to have a quick shower then I'm just going to grab my stuff and go, but first I need something to eat because there's nothing at my place either.

I get up, pull on a jumper and pad to the bathroom, another impersonal room. Gray even has his few personal items lined up on the side of the sink, though I suppose he's taken most of it with him. There's nothing in the cabinet above the sink.

I'm hungry and find half a loaf of dry bread in the kitchen, so I make myself toast. Even after two cups of coffee my headache is definitely starting to take hold and I need painkillers. I yank open a few cupboard doors looking for painkillers but there's nothing. I stuff my cup and plate into the dishwasher and wander back into Gray's bedroom. I check the bedside drawer on my side of the bed which is empty, then check Gray's which, at least, is not empty.

He has a few pens, a few coins, a phone charger, but no painkillers that I can see, not even one lonely paracetamol that has come loose from its packet. I pull the drawer further out, right out and lay it on the bed. Something catches my eye, something small and shiny.

A googly eye.

Now that's weird. Probably left behind by the previous tenant, a child perhaps.

I rummage a little more, there are bits of paper, a couple of receipts and then I find something so familiar that it makes my heart stop.

Yin.

Did I bring it here?

Did I leave it here?

Why would I do that? If I did bring it I would have put it in my bedside drawer, not his. Wouldn't I?

I grab it, hold it tight in my hand. Is it Adam's yin or just a similar one?

I hear rapid breathing, my own. My heart is beating out a sharp, staccato rhythm in my chest.

I rake around in the drawer again, find the googly eye, stick it in place on yin.

It's just too much of a coincidence.

How the hell did Gray get yin?

I must have brought it here.

I didn't bring it here.

I couldn't find it anywhere in Adam's flat and I certainly looked.

Did I find it and then forgot I found it?

Have I blanked it out? They say grief messes with your head, but this? It makes no sense. Gray has never been to Adam's flat. Not once. He doesn't even know where it is, so if it's not him who's brought it here, it must be me.

Why can't I remember?

I slump down on the bed and shake, all the while clutching yin to my chest.

I must be going mad.

The sound of an old-style phone, a landline, shakes me. My headache is still with me, pounding now. I stumble down to the kitchen to get a glass of water. I down several glasses.

There's a light flashing over on the sideboard by the dining table. It's an answerphone. Quaint. I've not noticed it before. Flashing means a message, I assume. I really shouldn't but I press play.

'Hi Mr Pershore, it's Shelley from Cleverley's. I've tried your mobile but you're not picking up and it's not going to voicemail so trying your landline now. We visited your flat in Cavendish Court on Saturday and….'

I slump to the floor as she goes on to give a valuation and says it will sell quickly as they already have several clients looking in that area who will definitely be interested.

That's my flat. He's had my flat valued before I have even agreed to selling it. Before he even suggested selling it to me.

How the hell did they get into my flat?

Gray must have a key.

But he didn't get it from me.

Or, at least, I didn't give it to him.

I ring for a taxi because thanks to Gray picking me up, I don't even have my car here.

☯☯☯

I don't get dressed, just grab my things, stuff them in my bag and leave. I have yin too.

The taxi driver barely looks at me, it's possible he sees a lot of women in their night clothes with coats thrown on top. I don't care anyway.

I'm still reeling from the answerphone message. It dawns on me that the agent must still have my key. I need that back, now.

I open my door and know immediately that someone has been here. Saturday's post has been picked up and put on the hall table. I snatch it up but it's just junk mail so I stomp through to the kitchen and throw it in my recycling bin.

As I shower and dress my mind is swirling. How the hell did Gray get my key? How the hell did Gray get yin. Is it definitely yin? I find the handbag which yang has been in ever since I took it up to London to show Adam, and fish it out. I slot yin and yang together. A perfect match just like they were on that day with Adam, my last visit to him. It's yin. Did I bring it back without realising? What other explanation is there?

If Gray has managed to make a copy of my key without my noticing has he also managed to get a copy of Adam's key? I don't have that key now because it's gone to the new owners. Anyway, George told me that it wasn't possible to copy the key, a new lock would have to be fitted instead. He also said that the locksmith told him it wasn't the first new lock he'd fitted at Adam's flat in recent months.

My phone pings; a message from Gray: *How are you doing, beautiful? Just about to go into a very boring meeting.*

I stare at the phone. I feel sick and confused. I drop the phone on the sofa and flop down next to it. My headache has finally gone thanks to the mega painkillers I took when I came home.

My mind is working overtime now trying to fathom just what is going on. I can imagine a plausible explanation for yin but not for my flat key, not for the valuation. I pick up my phone and google the estate agent. I ring the number and when it's finally answered I ask for Shelley. It takes a while for her to come to the phone.

'Hello,' she says, a smile in her voice.

I end the call. I hope she doesn't ring back. I rang to ask questions, to get my key back because I don't think Gray's had time to go and retrieve it. Maybe he doesn't need to because he could have had more than one cut.

My phone pings again. I hope it's not Gray. I hope it's not Shelley.

It's Jasper: *Gerard and I are over at his storage place sorting out Adam's paintings for his exhibition. Gerard has decided to bring it forward, or rather extend the length. We've had a lot of enquiries about it, so know the interest is definitely high.*

Great, I reply. *Thanks for all your help, both of you.*

You're welcome. But that wasn't the primary reason for me messaging you. We've discovered another painting. A small one. It was tucked into the bottom corner of a much larger piece. I think you're going to want to see it. Make sure you're sitting down.

His message is followed immediately by a photo.

I am sitting down but I have to jump up immediately and run to the bathroom to be sick – a rancid combination of coffee and toast. I'm sitting on the bathroom floor gasping and shaking when I hear my phone ringing. I crawl back on all fours because I cannot trust my shaky legs.

'Angie,' Jasper says. 'Are you all right? Did you get the picture?'

'Yes,' I croak.

'Are you okay?'

'Yes. Yes.' I take a deep breath and compose myself.

'Is it him? Do you think it's Perry?'

'Yes, it's definitely Perry,' I say, one-hundred percent confident that it is.

'What shall we do? We could go to the police.'

'Yes, maybe. In the meantime, could you courier it to me as soon as possible?'

He agrees he will and we end the call.

I message Gray: *Missing you. When will you be back?*

Friday about two, he replies. *Missing you too. Love you.*

I reply with a heart emoji.

Twenty-seven

It's Thursday afternoon when I arrive at Gray's in full daylight and park on the drive. It's a small drive only able to fit one car. So I'll have to move it before Gray gets back. I unload my bags.

Gray's place is exactly as I left it on Monday morning. I pick up his mail and drop it on the hall table. Then snatch it back up again, but there's nothing of interest, mostly advertising and junk. Shame that.

I've spent the last few days sorting things out, ensuring that there won't be any more impromptu estate agent visits. I've had the locks changed, there are three keys and I have them all. And they, like Adam's keys, cannot be copied. Three keys. I asked the locksmith if three keys are the norm and after he squinted at me as though I was mad, he said they were. So there were three keys to Adam's apartment. That's what we had after George had the lock changed, three keys. But I've checked with him and he said there were only two keys after Adam died, one on Adam's person and another in a kitchen drawer. That means there was one missing.

I've also steeled myself and opened the bag the police gave us, the one containing Adam's personal belongings. George had already checked everything he expected to be there was there – and taken the key out, obviously. Adam's phone was remarkably intact considering what had happened to it. Just a crack on one corner of the screen. Of course the battery was flat and I couldn't charge it, so I've brought it with me because maybe the charger in Gray's bedside table will fit it, a long shot but worth a try. I don't remember seeing a charger at Adam's.

His wallet was a bit more damaged, torn in half and dotted with what I assume is blood. There wasn't anything else. Inside his wallet he had seventeen pounds and some change. He had his debit card and, tucked away in the back of his wallet was his gold credit card, his *never to be used except in emergencies* card. The one that came with the big fat bill.

I unpack my bags. I have the makings for a lasagne, not exactly exciting but something I can do. I also have a couple of bottles of wine, a nice Barolo for Gray and a no-alcohol white fizz for me. I've got some fresh bread and some milk and I've bought a nice sickly pudding from M&S food hall. Gray has a sweet tooth so he'll enjoy that.

Once I've put everything away in the fridge and unpacked the rest of my bags I begin to explore his house. There are three bedrooms and I know Gray uses one of them as an office. I've not really been in there, just peered through the door when he's busy. The desk is some fancy minimalist thing that probably came with the house. I saunter in and plonk myself down at it. The surface is clear apart from a pen pot with three pens and a pencil in it. I try the drawers, there are three fairly small ones along the front. Two open easily, one with a few sheets of paper in it, all blank, and the other empty. The middle drawer is locked.

Not for long.

I empty out the pen pot and low and behold there's a key. It's exactly the place I would drop my key, in fact it's exactly what I do at work, what most people do.

It takes no time to open the drawer and now I see exactly why he keeps it locked. It's quite insulting really that he wasn't more careful with the key because he obviously thinks he's completely outwitted me. That I wouldn't think to even look.

Well, he's almost right, isn't he? Because if I hadn't had that headache, hadn't hunted for painkillers and found yin, then I wouldn't be doing this now. Or maybe I would after I'd seen that painting.

I take the contents out and line everything up along the desk. There are credit cards, six in fact, five have names I'm not familiar with, the other is Adam's, his emergency gold card. Except it's not because I have that back at my place inside his blood splattered wallet. This must be a copy, a clone. There are several passports too, all with pictures of Gray in them but with different names, different looks. I don't even know where you get stuff like this from, but Gray obviously does. There isn't one for his current name though, Graham Pershore, and there isn't one for Perry either. Perhaps he has them with him. Then there's the notebook. It's small and well-thumbed and as I flick through the pages I grin to myself. I can't quite believe my luck. Gray must think I am super thick and obviously, very trustworthy. He has listed all the credit cards together with their pin numbers on one page. On a separate page is a long list of bank accounts and passwords, many with crosses against them.

Not so clever then. But he thought it was safe, locked away in this drawer. And dumb little me would never suspect.

I sweep the credit cards and passports back into the

drawer. I wonder if, like Adam's, these are no longer working and he keeps them just as souvenirs?

Then I go and get my laptop from one of my bags.

It doesn't take me long to log into his bank accounts. I start with the bottom three, the ones with no crosses against them. Five accounts, different banks, different names. I whip the passports out of the drawer and compare them. Of course the names match. None for Graham Pershore though.

The amount of money spread across the accounts is mind boggling. Hundreds of thousands of pounds. As I scroll through I can see that most of the recent money, the money that makes up the bulk of the balances has come from one account. It's one of the accounts he's put a cross by. I try to open that but it comes up as not available. I assume the cross means he's closed the account.

Well, that won't be staying in your accounts, Gray, you can be sure of that.

I flex my fingers ready to do the evil deed when I stop. What if he has alerts on his phone for his online banking.

Damn it.

I don't want to forewarn him.

Getting the money back is the least of it.

I do need to check something though. In my bag I have a bank statement of Adam's which shows where his money was transferred to. My heart misses a beat when I see that it matches Gray's most recent account with a cross.

That must have been Perry's account. I wonder where Perry's passport is? I wonder if Gray is using it right now?

I close everything down on my laptop and shut it. Then I take it back into the living and put it back into my bag.

The daylight is starting to fade so I need to move my car. I go outside and make a great show of opening and closing the boot, slamming the doors, making it look as though I'm checking for something. I have to do this for several minutes until, eventually, a nosy neighbour pops his head out from behind the hedge.

'Everything all right?' he says.

'Yes, fine, thanks. Just looking for something. Found it now.'

He nods, he has a *thank God for that* expression on his face.

I get into the car and drive off, crunching the gears a little as I go. It's a small close and all the houses face each other, Gray says it's why he couldn't live anywhere like this permanently because everyone knows everyone else's business. He also doesn't like that there is a little path running down the side of his house. But today, that path will be my best friend.

Twilight comes quickly, soon followed by darkness. I drive around a little before parking my car in the road behind Gray's house. Then I skip up the path alongside his house and let myself in. I'm quiet, it's dark and I don't think anyone has seen me.

I hope.

I pull all the curtains closed and make sure I'm in the back of the house, the kitchen, not the front.

My phone pings and Gray messages me: So looking forward to being home tomorrow. It's been a long week. Missed you.

I don't reply. Instead picking up my phone and ringing him.

'I've missed you too,' I tell him.

We exchange sweet nothing talk for a few minutes,

then end the call. I've told him not to eat lunch before he gets back as I'm cooking something for us. He laughs. I don't think I've ever cooked him a meal.

I retrieve the charger from Gray's bedside table and try it in Adam's phone. Success. I wait a few minutes before turning it on.

I key in Adam's passcode and watch the phone spring to life. I don't doubt that Perry new Adam's passcode too, how else could he have deleted so many photos. I scroll through his contacts for Perry, ring, but Perry's number doesn't exist any longer. Not that I expected it to.

I find the dating app, the one where Adam had no success. He thought he was so lucky meeting Perry organically. Perry who didn't even know who Adam was.

I scroll through pictures of the men who swiped Adam, the ones he didn't swipe back. I know what I'm looking for and I find it quickly. Even though I was expecting this it still takes my breath away.

I fetch my own phone, find the dating app I met Gray on and scroll through for his picture.

If there was ever any doubt in my mind it's completely gone now. The only difference between the photo of Gray on my phone and the one on Adam's is the hair. Long on Adam's, very short on mine. But on Adam's phone his hair isn't blonde and his name isn't Perry.

I'm bored now.

I can't do anything else.

I can't even go home because then I would have to return in the daylight and I don't want to do that. Officially, I'm not here.

I pull out the letter from my handbag. I'm telling Gray that we're over. I reread it before dropping it back in my handbag. For all the things I could say I'm not saying much, just that I think I've made a mistake and I don't want to marry him. Then I wish him a happy life and luck in finding his soulmate in the future.

Nice touch that.

I turn my phone off.

And Adam's, and make a mental note to call and cancel his contract. I really should have done it sooner but it's worked to my advantage. As an executor of Adam's will George had transferred all the direct debits into a temporary account – the utilities still had to be paid.

I make myself some toast, turn on the kitchen TV, a tiny thing in the corner, and flick through rubbish channels before finally turning it off.

I go to bed at nine-thirty and sleep surprising well. It's not fully daylight when I awake so I go around and open all the curtains. This house is at the end of the close, facing down the street and not directly onto other houses, so hopefully no one has noticed the movement of the curtains – I just didn't want anyone seeing a chink of light at night.

I shower and dress and eat some breakfast and tidy up before I make the lasagne. Once done I set it aside. It will go in the oven at about one-thirty, and it will be perfectly cooked in time for Gray's arrival.

Around noon I open the Barolo to let it breathe.

I'm standing in the front window, hiding behind the semi-closed blinds when I see Gray pull up. I dart back into the kitchen and await his arrival.

This is going to be fun; I tell myself.

I hope.

Twenty-eight

'Hi Angie,' Gray calls, closing the door behind him. He drops his bags on the hall floor before striding into the kitchen and rushing towards me. He looks genuinely pleased to see me.

We hug. It's sort of nice. Shame that.

'Something smells good.'

'Are you hungry?'

'Starving. The hotel breakfast today was so so.'

'I've got a nice bottle of Barolo breathing…' I flash my eyes and grin.

'Mmm, sounds good. Pour me a glass and I'll be back in a minute.' He heads upstairs with his bag. When he comes back he's changed out of his work clothes. He looks comfortable, relaxed.

I hand him his wine glass and take a sip of my own.

He takes a sip and I await his verdict.

'That's good,' he says. 'Just what I need right now.'

'Tough week?'

'Yeah. Isn't work always tough?' He takes another sip. 'Feels very decadent sipping red wine in the middle of the day.'

'Doesn't it.' I laugh. 'Sit down, food's ready.'

As he sits he notices my bags in the corner of the

kitchen. 'Oh, you've moved in?' He grins.

'Not completely,' I say, smiling. 'Just brought some things over to start with.'

'Cool.' He takes another sip of his wine, then evidently enjoying it, finishes the glass. 'Thought any more about selling your place?'

'Still thinking.' I grab the bottle and fill his glass again.

'Hey, you'll be getting me drunk.'

'That's the plan.' I giggle.

I fill my own glass and he doesn't even notice that it's alcohol free. But then, why would he?

We eat our food, we giggle because one of us is getting very intoxicated, and afterwards, at my insistence, Gray retires to the living room while I clear our dishes away. I stack the dishwasher and put it on.

I sit down next to Gray on the sofa with a filled glass of non-wine. His glass is empty, fortunately I've brought the bottle of Barolo and what remains of its contents in with me. I top up Gray's glass.

'That's a good wine,' he says, after taking another sip. 'Was it expensive?'

'Fairly.'

He leans back and closes his eyes. I gently nudge him in the ribs. I don't want him falling asleep on me in here.

'Sorry,' he says. 'Been such a long week.'

'Why don't we snuggle down in bed then.' I wink at him. He grins back. 'Then if you fall asleep it won't matter.'

'I won't fall asleep.' He gets up, grabs his wine glass and holds out a hand for me.

Hand in hand we walk up to the bedroom.

Gray disappears into the bathroom while I quickly slip my clothes off, pull on a new nightdress – one I know Gray is going to love – spray some perfume around and arrange a few other things.

Gray's a long time. I hope he hasn't fallen asleep. I knock on the door.

'Are you okay?' I ask.

'Fine, just cleaning my teeth.' He opens the door dabbing at his face with a towel. 'Mmm, like it,' he says, leering at me.

I take his hand and lead him to the bed, help him undress and we both climb in.

'That wine must be strong,' he says. 'I swear I can't feel my tongue.' His eyes close again as he snuggles down.

'It's not the wine.'

He opens his eyes and frowns at me. I grin. I can tell how tired he is because his lazy eye is starting to wander.

'What the fuck…?' he yells, finally seeing it.

'What?'

'That.' He lifts a finger to point at the picture I've put up on the wall at the end of the bed.

I turn my gaze towards the portrait. 'It's one of my brother's.'

Even in the dim light of the bedroom I can see Gray's face turning paler and paler.

'Aren't you going to ask me who it is?'

He looks at me as though he doesn't understand what I'm saying. And that may be the case, although I hope not. Not yet.

'It's Perry.' I watch Gray's face for a reaction but he just blinks several times. Perry's handsome face stares down at us, his blond hair flowing out behind him. Adam has done an amazing job, even managing to catch Perry's squint whilst also making it look attractive. 'You remember the day Adam died?'

'What?'

‘I saw you on the platform. Saw Adam catch up with you.’

‘What are you talking about?’ He really doesn’t sound very convincing.

‘I saw you on the platform. Are you having trouble understanding me? Sorry about that.’ I giggle again. ‘You see, I had raced up to see Adam that day because Jasper had sent me a frantic message about Perry going missing and Adam being in a hell of a state.’ I wait for a reaction but he just stares at me.

‘It was pure luck that I was right there in that Tube station at that time. Amazing and coincidental. I was on my way to Adam’s when I saw him leap over the ticket barrier. I couldn’t believe my eyes. He never travels on the Tube, not any public transport really, so doesn’t have an Oyster card which was why he had to leap the barrier. I knew it must be serious for him to be down there, he’s not overly fond of crowded public places. Then he was shouting your name, well, Perry, not Gray. He caught up with you eventually on the platform. You were wearing a silly hat, a baby blue fluffy thing, not that I could see your face properly because you weren’t looking my way. You must have shaved the blond off by then. Do you remember how short your hair was when I met you for the first time in person and you’d just started growing your beard? But Adam still recognised you, didn’t he? He touched you on the shoulder but you pushed him away.’

‘He lost his footing,’ Gray says, attempting to pull himself up. ‘I didn’t kill him.’

‘I know you didn’t. But it was your fault.’

Gray gulps. I’m not sure if he’s trying to get more air into his lungs or if it’s just shock or if his lungs are packing up.

‘You as good as killed him with what you did to him

though, didn't you? Scammed him. Took his money. You ruined everything between me and Adam. We used to be so close and you spoiled that just so you could scam his money off him. I was so angry with Adam for being so stupid. I still am.'

Gray makes another attempt to pull himself up.

'Don't bother,' I tell him, resting my hand on his shoulder. 'I suspect you won't be getting up again. Ever.'

'What have you done to me?'

'Wined and dined you.' I laugh. 'You like doing that too, don't you? You took Adam all over the place, Sweden, Scotland, Amsterdam. He thought you were so generous but he was paying for it all along.'

'I paid in the beginning,' he says, sounding indignant. It makes me laugh.

'Did you? Or did you use someone else's cloned card. How many more were there? Have you got someone else on the go at the moment? Were you going to clean me out then move on to the next one? Male or female?'

He opens his mouth then closes it.

'Say something. Please,' I implore, before laughing.

'I didn't want him dead.'

'Ahh, of course not. You'll be saying you loved him next. You'll be telling me you love me, again.'

'I do.' Little tears trickle from the sides of his eyes. I don't know if this is his trick or they are genuine.

'I don't think you do. You love yourself and you love money, other people's money. You have no feelings at all for anyone else, do you? You're quite the psychopath.'

'We could still have a good life together, you and I,' he says. 'You could ring an ambulance; tell them I've accidently overdosed or something. You could save me.'

I laugh. 'Bless you, you never give up, do you?'

After surveying me for a moment or two he changes

tack. 'How long have you known?'

'Oh, I'm almost as dim as you think.' I laugh again, quite a cackle, anyone would think I'd been drinking. 'I didn't recognise you from the platform. I saw you; I knew you were Perry because Adam called out to you, but I couldn't see your face properly. You're very good, you really do look quite different. The blond hair, the Swedish persona, what's that about?'

He looks away.

'I found out on Monday.'

'That fucking picture.'

'No, that was confirmation, the tipping point. It was yin. And maybe the estate agent ringing up with a valuation for my flat made me a bit suspicious. So several things, but the painting was definitely the confirmation.'

'Yin?' He screws his face up so much that I wonder if what I've given him is wearing off.

I leap up off the bed. 'Don't go anywhere,' I say, with a giggle before returning with my handbag. 'This is yin and this is yang, Adam had yin and I had yang.' I hold the stones up in front of him, fitting them together. 'I hunted high and low for yin in Adam's flat then found it by accident in your bedside drawer. Bit careless there, weren't you? I was looking for painkillers for my headache after you left on Monday. Never would have found it otherwise. Even when I did, I still had my doubts.'

He attempts to shake his head, his eyes bulging with the effort.

'Then Jasper sent me a photo of this painting they'd found; it was tucked into the back of one of his bigger pieces. Well, there was that cute little squint you get when you're tired.' I lean over and stroke his eye; he attempts to pull away from me but can't. 'When I was hunting around your house, this house, God knows how many others you have, I found another one of Adam's paintings in the back of a wardrobe. Jasper said he thought one was missing. So, that's a bonus. Don't worry, I'm taking it with me.'

'You won't get away with this. You can't just kill someone.'

I ignore his outburst because I think it's important that he knows how I caught him out, not that he's going to learn from it. It's too late for that.

'Anyway, where was I?' I tuck yin and yang back into my handbag and pull out a little bag of powder, flapping it in his face. 'Oh, this is what you've taken. It's a right mixture of painkillers and some pills I had for depression after Adam died and well, all sorts. I used that cute little mortar and pestle I found in one of your cupboards to grind it all down. Took me ages, but so worth it. Put it in the wine and hey, here we are. I'm just going to leave it in the kitchen, half open.' I take a tissue and wipe it down, then pick up Gray's hand and dab his fingerprints all over it.

'Bitch,' he mutters. 'Ring an ambulance, save me. We can have fun together.'

'Not going to happen. You see when you took my brother for a fool you broke his heart. And you broke mine. And my family's. He'd have given you anything, he had plenty of money and the potential to earn plenty more. You could have had a good life with Adam, but no, you scammed him. That's what I can't forgive. Then not content with what you had you sought me out and romanced me so you could get the rest. It's ironic really, Adam was always the clever one, yet you fooled him better than you fooled me.'

'Save me,' he says. He's crying properly now and I

think it's genuine.

'No can do. Sorry. Not sorry.' I stand up. 'Don't go yet, got to get some things.'

When I come back he's staring off into the distance and he doesn't look at me. He can't have gone yet, I haven't finished.

'Perry,' I say, and he glances at me. 'Thank God for that, I thought you'd gone.' I plonk the drawer from his desk on the bed, together with my laptop. 'See I found your little treasure trove. You really should have kept that key in a safer place. Don't you know that everyone keeps their desk key in their pen pot?' I tut for effect before tipping the contents out. 'All these passports. Where do you get them? Don't answer that, it's a rhetorical question. Ditto the cards, all cloned?'

I open my laptop and use the details in his notebook to open his bank accounts.

'I want you to see this because I think it's important that you have closure, that we both do.' I type away moving his money around and then show him the results. 'There, all gone into my account. Where it should have been immediately after Adam died.'

'You won't get away with it.'

'Well you have, for years I suspect. Anyway, you don't need to worry about that.'

'Save me,' he pleads again.

'It's not going to happen. And it's not as though the police will know about your bank accounts, will they, because I have the only record.' I tip the credit cards, the passports and the little notebook into my handbag then take the drawer back to his desk where I give the whole lot a good polish.

When I come back I see that he's managed to move himself a little, his head is flopping over towards the bedside table.

'Oh dear,' I say, propping him back up. 'Let's make you more comfortable.

'Save me,' he mutters, his voice really quiet.

'No.'

'You won't get away with it.'

'I will. Because you don't really exist, do you? I've no idea who you are. And I realise I don't really care. Ah, that reminds me, just need to check your bag.' I stride over to where he's left it on the chair in the corner and open it. There are the shirts and clean clothes he took away on Monday and none of them have been worn. So, wherever he's been he didn't need these clothes. I fish around in the bag until I find his passport, Perry Oblekt. 'Here it is.' I wave it around before slipping it into my handbag. I take his laptop from the bag too, wouldn't want the police inspecting that.

'They'll know it's murder, why would I kill myself? They'll know it's you.'

'Oh, yes, thank you, I'd almost forgotten. The letter.' I fish around in my handbag for the letter I've written him breaking off our engagement. I rip it open and read it out. '*Sorry but I realise that I don't love you enough so I can't go through with it. I hope you understand. I wish you a happy life blah blah.* Do you like that bit? I've just signed it A. I slip off my engagement ring and drop it into the envelope. 'Shame I can't keep that, it looks expensive, but it wouldn't look real otherwise, would it? Maybe the police will give it back to me.' I chuckle.

'You're mad.'

'I'm very mad. Mad at you for what you've done. Mad at my brother for falling for it. Mad at myself for almost falling for it. But now you only have yourself to blame.' I take his hand and press his prints onto the letter, then

I crumple it up and leave it with the envelope on the bed. 'Nice touch that, don't you think?'

He grunts because he can't do much else.

'Will you be all right for five minutes? I just need to empty the dishwasher and pack my bags before I leave.'

'H-e-l-p m-e,' he slurs.

'Back soon,' I murmur, rushing off to the kitchen.

It doesn't take me long to tidy up, put the dishes away, gather up any evidence. I polish the wine bottle clean of my prints then take it back up to Gray's bedroom. He's slumped further down the bed. Has he gone? Have I missed it? I use his hands to fingerprint the bottle then let it fall to the floor. The dregs seep out onto the carpet.

He grunts.

'Ah, you're still here. Well, that's fine because I can't leave yet. Can't go until it's properly dark. Won't be long. Ah, there it is, nearly forgot.' I lean over and grab his phone from the bedside table.

As expected there are notifications from his many banking apps informing him of all the transfers. I'm so glad I exercised patience and waited. I delete the notifications, then delete the apps. Then I send myself a message pleading with me not to leave him.

'That's better.' I give his phone a quick wipe, then press the phone into his hand to ensure his prints are on it. He has no grip left at all. Then I let the phone fall onto the floor. 'There, isn't that good?'

He gasps. Is this his last? 'Help me.'

'No.'

He uses all his effort to force out his next words, even so, it takes him ages to say it. 'I didn't kill Adam. Save me. You're not a murderer.'

'Ahh, bless you. I know you didn't kill Adam. It was just a little shove really, a bit like when we were kids and used to play fight. But, like I said, I was so angry with him for being so stupid and for freezing me out, that I might have pushed a little harder than I should.'

His eyes widen and I pat his shoulder.

'I know you didn't kill Adam, because I did. So I am a murderer. Or maybe his death was manslaughter. Not premeditated. Not planned. Not like yours.' I smile at him. 'Your death is my debt to Adam. We always used to say we'd die for each other, but I think killing is a better show of love, don't you? And it's all your own fault. If only you hadn't been such a thieving little shit.'

Twenty-nine

It was after midnight before I could leave.

It took him that long to finally succumb. At one point I seriously considered giving him a bit more but I didn't think he'd be able to swallow it. Then I considered smothering him, but they'd be able to tell, wouldn't they, during the post mortem?

So I just sat there, chatting away. Telling him about the happy childhood Adam and I had had. He didn't react, not so much as a grunt. But he did keep on breathing.

Eventually his breathing slowed down, really slowed down until I thought that was it, but then he gasped another breath in. I told him that at least he was going peacefully and that he wasn't dying a death of a thousand cuts like he'd inflicted, metaphorically, on Adam, and countless others no doubt. I told him I was performing a public service really, stopping him ruining any more lives.

After he'd finally stopped breathing I had to wait for his body to go cold just to make sure. Not very nice, but there you are, if you do these things you have to see them through to the grisly end.

Then I checked I had everything, gathered up my bags

and left. I scuttled down the path beside the house so grateful that its position made it almost impossible to see from the street. Then I dumped my bags in my car and went home.

I don't think anyone saw me. That road behind Gray's is quiet and there are only two houses and they're at the far end, the rest of it is filled with overgrown trees.

It took the police nearly three weeks to find him. No one missed him, or at least no one who knew where he was missed him. It was one of his neighbours who raised the alarm when they noticed that the bedroom curtains were drawn all the time but the bathroom light was on permanently. Nice touch that, I think.

It took the police another four weeks to track me down. They found me at my parents' place, we were eating Sunday dinner. Everyone was there, including George. Christmas had been and gone and we'd all tried to have a nice time even though we missed Adam terribly.

I'd told the family, almost in passing, about the engagement and how I'd returned the ring. But that was it, I'd never mentioned Gray again. Neither did anyone else. They didn't miss him because they weren't expecting to see him. Mum might have said it was a shame, but that was it.

Everyone was shocked and everyone said it was terribly sad. I cried when the police told me, it was expected. I said I was so sorry that he'd done that just because I broke it off with him.

I wasn't though.

He deserved it.

I never mentioned Perry, or Adam. It wouldn't be good to connect them to Gray.

Jasper and Gerard are doing a sterling job of selling

Adam's paintings. Prices are premium naturally. Jasper never met Gray – you can't count a fleeting glance across a crowded room at Adam's funeral – so has never joined the dots. Or if he has he's never said anything to me. Although I doubt he would pair the two together, Gray looked so very different from Perry really, aside from the squint.

I don't know what happened to his body and have no idea what the funeral arrangements were. The police never told me.

And I've never heard any more from the police about what happened to Adam's money. Doubt I ever will.

Not that it matters now, because I have it all back.

Just a shame that Adam had to die for it.

On the days when I feel guilty about Adam's death – yes, I do have them – I console myself with the fact that without Adam's death I'd never have caught and punished Perry. I've probably saved countless others from falling for his thieving, scamming charms.

I also have a lovely original Adam Hames RA painting, one of his last, one of his best.

I'll hang it pride of place in my new, rather grand, home once I move.

The other painting, which I like to think of as Adam's labour of love, is in a suitcase under my bed, together with some credit cards, a laptop and a little notebook.

I'll have a ceremonial bonfire when I move house.

THE END

Someone's lying. Is it her husband or her best friend?

Recurring dreams of a car crash make sleep a nightmare for Juliette but the real nightmare begins when she wakes up. Her devoted husband Robin stays by her side, determined to help her remember how her whole world was turned upside down.

He's the love of her life and he's vowed he will never leave her and he's true to his word. But, there are things that Robin doesn't know so she turns to her best friend Stephen to find out the truth. He's the brother she never had and they've been best friends since childhood. He knows her like no one else, not even Robin.

As Juliette's memory begins to return she starts to doubt her own sanity and is forced to ask herself – do we ever really know the people we love?

She's thirty-five and starting afresh. What's wrong with that?

Absolutely nothing. After ten, fun filled years in London, Zoe Tydeman has returned to the sleepy Wiltshire village of her childhood. She's bought a house, got herself a lovely new job in a craft shop, and she's finally growing up and moving on. She's put behind her the mistakes of the past and life is now sunshine and smiles.

Until a pink envelope lands on her doormat. 'Save the Date' has never hurt so much. Her best friends are getting married. A love she hoped would fizzle out has become permanent, very permanent. Where exactly does that leave Zoe? A singleton at the kids' table, that's where.

Will Zoe get over her unrequited love? Can she forgive her friends? Is it time to stop wasting time and get over herself? Join Zoe on her quest to get a life – of her own.

The hot guy upstairs thinks she's an idiot in a frog onesie…

Ella Taylor is having a tough time:
•Her mum's recently died
•She's been cheated out of a promotion at work
•Her new boss is a Barbie doll who models herself on Gwyneth Paltrow
•She's living in a horrible bedsit

And now she's inherited a rundown cottage in a hick village with a bunch of conditions attached.

If you're a fan of Sophie Kinsella, Sophie Ranald or Portia Mactintosh, or just love a quirky British romcom, you'll love this!

Sequel to laugh-out-loud romantic comedy Blame it on the Onesie

Pull on your onesie, light the fire, grab a hot chocolate and join Ella, Nathan, Sam, Charlie, Walt and the cavalry for another riotous read.

It's all change for Ella.
•Nathan has declared his love: 'It was only ever you I wanted, only ever you I loved.'
•Sleaze weasel Hal is but a distant memory
•Spring Cottage 'rules' are getting in the way
•And Christmas seems a long way off

There will be weirdness, love and laughter... you have been warned.

Printed in Great Britain
by Amazon

85446458R00150